THE GECKO & STICKY

VILLAIN'S LAIR

Also by Wendelin Van Draanen

WENDELIN VAN DRAANEN

THE GECKO & STICKY
VILLAIN'S LAIR

ILLUSTRATED BY
STEPHEN GILPIN

ALFRED A. KNOPF   NEW YORK

For the superhero educators in Bakersfield and Lamont,

and for the kids there who reach for the power inside.

You are *asombrrrrroso*!

THIS IS A BORZOI BOOK PUBLISHED BY ALFRED A. KNOPF

Visit us on the Web! www.randomhouse.com/kids

Educators and librarians, for a variety of teaching tools,
visit us at www.randomhouse.com/teachers

Library of Congress Cataloging-in-Publication Data
Van Draanen, Wendelin.
The Gecko and Sticky : Villain's Lair / by Wendelin Van Draanen ;
illustrations by Stephen Gilpin. — 1st ed.
p. cm. — (The Gecko and Sticky)
Summary: Thirteen-year-old Dave and his sidekick, a talking gecko named Sticky, try to retrieve
an ancient Aztec powerband and its magic ingots from the evil villain Damien Black.
ISBN 978-0-375-84376-1 (trade) — ISBN 978-0-375-94567-0 (lib. bdg.)
[1. Adventure and adventurers—Fiction. 2. Magic—Fiction. 3. Geckos—Fiction. 4. Lizards—Fiction. 5.
Humorous stories.] I. Gilpin, Stephen, ill. II. Title. III. Title: Villain's lair.
PZ7.V2857Ge 2009
[Fic]—dc22
2008012377

Printed in the United States of America
February 2009
10 9 8 7 6 5 4 3 2 1

First Edition

CONTENTS

Chapter 1
THE OOZY, STINKY CAVE

"Quick, *señor*, hide in there!" Sticky said, pointing past dangling moss into the deep blackness of a cave.

"That's even worse than out here!" Dave whispered.

"Not if Damien Black sees you," Sticky warned.

Dave Sanchez looked at the forest behind them, his heart beating madly. From the tales Sticky had told him, Damien Black was ruthless. Evil. A treasure hunter who would stop at nothing to get what he wanted.

But had the noise in the night been him?

Had Damien seen them hide the bike and squeeze past his gate?

The treasure hunter's mansion loomed like a monster above them. Even washed in moonlight it looked dark. Eerie. The sort of spooky house you see only in your very worst nightmares: pointed spires, shutters hanging from a single hinge, bats fluttering around the belfry . . .

Not that this house *had* a belfry, but you get the idea.

What this nightmarish mansion *did* have (besides pointed spires and shutters hanging from a single hinge) were rooms that jutted out at odd angles. Rooms that seemed almost suspended in space.

These rooms had either no windows, or unusually shaped windows, up very high.

Some of the rooms had ladders mounted on the outside.

Ladders that seemed to lead nowhere.

Others had cables or pulleys or winches, or really, just turning-pulling-cranking thingamajigs. It was hard to imagine what they were used for.

Were they torture chambers?

Dastardly plotting-to-take-over-the-world chambers?

Or perhaps these rooms held vast amounts of evilly acquired treasure.

Chests of gold!

Maps to riches!

The pearls, diamonds, and emeralds of kings!

Anyone would agree it was odd.

Very odd indeed.

"*Señor*, in there!" Sticky said again, and this time he tugged Dave's ear with one hand as he pointed into the cave with the other.

Dave hated when Sticky tugged his ear, but Sticky knew no other way to get Dave to listen. Sticky was, after all, just a gecko lizard, where Dave was a stubborn, all-knowing thirteen-year-old boy.

Something crunched through the darkness of the forest, and this time Dave followed the tug on his ear until he was safe inside the mossy cave.

Safe! Now, that's a laugh. They had stepped from the forest surrounding Damien Black's nightmarish mansion into a cave *beneath* his nightmarish mansion. A deep, dark cave that held, among other things, all the bats that would have been in the belfry, had there been one.

Not that Dave could see the bats yet. It was, as I have said, a deep, *dark* cave. And, as it turns out, smelly, too.

"Ay-ay-ay!" Sticky said, fanning the air in front of his face.

"I wish I'd brought a flashlight!" Dave whispered.

"How about matches?" Sticky asked.

"Matches? Where am I gonna get matches?"

"Hold on, *hombre*," Sticky said, then scurried over Dave's shoulder and into the backpack Dave wore everywhere.

So how *did* matches come to be inside Dave's backpack without him knowing it?

The same way that money or jewelry or, say, *grapes* would mysteriously appear in Dave's backpack: Sticky had put them there.

You see, Sticky was, on the whole, a good gecko. But he was a good gecko with a very bad habit.

He stole things.

Lifted them.

Snagged them!

He had, if you will, sticky fingers.

"It's not my fault, *hombre*," he would tell Dave. "I was born this way!"

Which is true; geckos have incredibly sticky fingers. And on this particular night, in this particular darkness, Sticky's bad habit happened to come in quite handy.

"Here, *hombre*," Sticky said, holding the box of matches up to Dave's face.

"How'd these get in my backpack?" Dave asked, taking them from him.

"You don't want to know," Sticky replied.

This was also true. Anytime Sticky would start to answer that question, Dave would say, "Stop! Don't tell me! I don't want to know!"

Dave did not ask again. Instead, he struck a match. But as the match flared to life, the boy and the gecko saw that they had entered a foul and fiendish cave that had oozing walls and . . .

"Bats!" Sticky cried, diving for cover inside Dave's sweatshirt.

Dave did not like bats either, but he had nowhere to dive. He did, however, have a match. A match that, just before it burned his fingers, cast enough light on the cave wall to reveal a mounted torch.

"Ouch!" Dave said, waving out the match.

"Did a bat bite you?" Sticky shouted from inside Dave's sweatshirt.

"No." Dave struck another match. "The *match* bit me."

Sticky emerged from the sweatshirt and asked, "Why is there a torch on the wall of an oozy, stinky cave?"

"I don't know," Dave said, pulling it out of its holder. He lit the torch with the match, and as he moved deeper into the cave, he wondered the exact same thing that Sticky had asked.

Why *was* there a torch on the wall of an oozy, stinky cave?

It's a well-known fact that bats are not comfortable with light *or* smoke, and since the torch was giving off a great deal of both, they were really coming to life now, fluttering about in the spooky, choppy way that bats do.

"I don't think bats eat geckos," Dave said, aware of the way Sticky was cowering inside his sweatshirt again.

"You don't *think, señor?*" Sticky asked.

But Dave did not answer. He was too busy noticing that this oozy, stinky cave had a passageway.

A passageway that led away from the stench and the dangling moss and the fluttery bats.

A passageway that led, Dave would soon learn, to somewhere much, much worse.

Chapter 2
PERHAPS YOU'RE WONDERING...

Perhaps you're wondering what Dave and Sticky were doing, creeping through a frightening forest and an oozy, stinky cave toward the underbelly of a nightmarish mansion.

Or perhaps you're wondering in what make-believe world a kleptomaniacal talking gecko lizard exists.

These are, I admit, perfectly understandable things to wonder.

Unfortunately, the explanation is not an easy one. You see, this story does not take place in a make-believe world, with make-believe villains and make-believe lizards.

This story is quite real.

Quite *true*.

And perhaps your reaction to this is, Impossible! Lizards can't talk!

That, too, would be a perfectly understandable reaction, and it happens to be the exact reaction Dave had when Sticky spoke to *him* for the first time.

Not that Sticky had spoken to him right away. Even though Dave had saved him from the clutches of a neighbor's cat, and had proclaimed him "the coolest lizard ever!" this was not enough to begin a conversation.

Nor was the fact that Dave let him roam freely through the humble apartment that Dave shared with his parents and little sister. Or that Dave took him everywhere. After all, geckos are known to bring good luck, so why not?

No, Sticky was more than just cautious.

He was afraid for his life.

Why?

Because he was hiding from more than just the neighbor's sharp-clawed cat.

He was hiding from a diabolical man named Damien Black.

It should have been enough to escape this evil treasure hunter's clutches with his life, but Sticky had managed to escape with something more, and Damien Black wanted it back.

Badly.

It should also have been enough for Sticky to hide in the safety of Dave's apartment for the rest of his life, but Damien Black still had something that *Sticky* wanted.

Maybe just as badly.

Sticky didn't want it for himself. He more wanted to get it away from Damien Black. After all, *he* was the one who had discovered the treasure, *he* was the one who had risked his life, *he* was the one who had brought it out of the realm of legend, back into the hands of man.

Now, you're probably wondering, What is this "it"?

And again, the answer is not an easy one. Or is, at the very least, not one you won't say "Impossible!" to when you hear. (Which means that you *will*, most likely, say "Impossible!")

So I am somewhat hesitant in sharing that what Sticky retrieved from an ancient Aztec treasure hidden for hundreds of years in the folds of a secret cavern was . . . a wristband.

A *magic* wristband, known also as a powerband.

Ah-ah-ah, I warned you. But as I've said before, this story is true.

Amazing?

Yes.

Incredible?

Yes.

But still, true.

Now, had this amazingly, incredibly magic

Aztec wristband worked on Sticky, he might have cut Damien out of the equation entirely. (After all, what had Damien done, really, but take him to the vast, unforgiving mountain where legend said the powerband had vanished?)

But the powerband did not work on Sticky.

And, as it turned out, it did not work by itself either.

You see, the wristband was but half of the equation.

The power ingots were the other.

These power ingots could easily be mistaken for ancient Aztec coins. What gives them away to the discerning eye, however, is that they are notched.

And have odd pictures on them.

And are shinier than gold.

Blindingly so.

In fact, you could pick them out of a treasure chest, no problem.

Assuming, of course, you were looking for shiny notched coins with strange pictures on them.

Which Sticky was.

Because Damien had told him to.

But let's go back to the wristband, shall we? That will take us back to Dave's reaction to Sticky being able to talk, which will take us back to what in the world these two were doing, creeping through a frightening forest and an oozy, stinky cave toward the underbelly of a nightmarish mansion.

Well, you've almost certainly figured that last bit out on your own by now, but I'll tell you anyway:

Damien Black still had the ingots.

Sticky had snagged the wristband.

The wristband is useless without the ingots.

The ingots are useless without the wristband.

Together, though, that's another story! By clicking a power ingot into a slot on the wristband, the wearer immediately possesses that particular ingot's particular power. Super-strength, lightning speed, invisibility . . . that sort of thing. It's a one-power-at-a-time sort of magic wristband, but still, very cool indeed.

Now, Damien had promised Sticky the life of a king if he could bring the powerband and the ingots out of the cavern, but in the end, Damien had betrayed him. Tricked him. And then, much worse, *caged* him. He was, Sticky learned the hard way, a beastly barracuda of a man. A bwaa-ha-ha-ha-in-the-night sort of villain. Damien did not care about Sticky. He merely saw him as a possession. A unique kind of treasure. Something he did not want to let get away.

But Damien Black underestimated the price

he would pay for his betrayal. For although it took all of Sticky's ingenuity and strength, he managed to escape the dastardly treasure hunter's lair with Damien's most valuable possession:

The magic wristband.

So! Knowing this now, you can see why it took a while for Sticky to work up the courage to talk to Dave. He liked the boy, but what if he was just another, younger Damien Black? What if he, too, would betray him and *cage* him?

But in the end, Sticky decided that getting his hands on the power ingots was not something he could do alone. He needed help, and Dave seemed just the boy to give it. He was strong and nimble and fast on a bike. He was old enough to go places on his own, and young enough to not freak out over a talking gecko lizard.

Or so Sticky hoped, anyway.

He really, really, really didn't want Dave to freak out.

Chapter 3
DAVE FREAKS OUT

It happened one afternoon when Dave was home alone. Sticky simply crawled onto his shoulder and said, *"Buenas tardes, señor!"*

"What?" Dave said, looking at the gecko with wide eyes.

"You heard me, *hombre*," Sticky said as he cocked his head. "I said, *'Buenas tardes.'* You know, good afternoon?"

"I know what *buenas tardes* means! But . . . but . . . you *talk?*"

"Looks like," Sticky said with a shrug, implying that Dave was brainy like a burro.

Dave shook out one ear.

He shook out the other.

"It's impossible!" he whispered, trying to convince himself that he wasn't hearing what he was indeed hearing. He looked at Sticky and said, "Talk again."

"What do you want me to say, *señor?*"

Dave fell into a chair. "A talking lizard!"

"A talking leeezard," Sticky repeated, pronouncing "lizard" the only way his accent would allow.

"A talking lizard!" Dave said again, and although Dave was much, much larger than Sticky, he looked enormously frightened.

"A talking leeezard!" Sticky repeated again, and although Sticky was much, much smaller than Dave, he looked enormously amused. .

Dave sat up a little. "How can you be talking? Are you enchanted? Bewitched? *Cursed?*"

Sticky shrugged. "I'm just me, *señor.*"

"Have you always been able to talk?" Dave asked, his voice but a whisper.

Sticky nodded his little gecko head and grinned. "*Sí, señor.* Ever since I can remember."

"Can *all* lizards talk?"

"*Ay caramba,* don't I wish? No! I've tried to teach them, but they look at me like my head's full of *loco* berries! I say to them, 'Theees is how you do it, seeee? You move your leeeeeps. You push words ouuuuuut.' But they won't even try! All they want to do is eat bugs and sleep."

"Eat bugs and sleep," Dave said, like he was in a trance.

"*Sí, señor.* So what was I supposed to do? Hang around a bunch of sleepy-eyed cricket catchers for the rest of my life? No way, José! I needed to shake a tail! Flap a tongue! Find someplace where I belonged!"

Dave's eyes were enormous. "And . . . and . . . you belong *here?*"

Sticky's face scrunched to one side.

His eyes became a bit shifty.

He inspected the fingernails of his little gecko hand.

And just when it seemed he would huff on his nails and buff them against his chest, he put the hand down and muttered, "That depends on you, *señor.*"

"On me?"

"*Sí.* On whether you're willing to help me."

"Help you?" Dave asked helplessly. "Help you how?"

"Ay-ay-ay," Sticky said. "This is not easy to explain."

Dave stared at the lizard for a moment, then said, "Well, try!"

Sticky tapped his little gecko chin with a little gecko finger and murmured, "*Dios mío*, where to begin?" But then, with great gecko wisdom, he decided that the very best place to begin was . . . at the beginning.

Now, as Sticky told Dave about Damien Black and the ancient Aztec powerband, and the vast, unforgiving mountain where he had so selflessly risked life and limb, he did it in a very *spicy* way, generously seasoning the story with expressions that were neither English nor Spanish, nor even Spanglish. Expressions like "Holy tacarole!" and "Freaky *frijoles!*" and "Chony baloney!"

Expressions that, really, could only be called one thing:

Stickynese.

In fact, the telling of the tale became *so* spiced that as Sticky was explaining the power of each magic ingot, Dave could take it no longer. He jumped up and said, "Stop! I don't believe you! Not for a minute! There's no such thing as a wrist-band that can make you fly! Or turn you invisible! Or let you walk up walls! It's impossible!"

Sticky pursed his lips.

He cocked his head.

His whole mouth screwed around from one side of his face to the other.

And at long last he said, "You cut me to the quick, *señor*. I am most insulted. Perhaps you are not the one to help me after all." Then he jumped off of Dave's shoulder and scurried across Dave's bedroom, vanishing behind a small bookcase.

Dave cried, "Wait!" because although he knew a magic wristband was an impossibility, so, too, was a talking gecko lizard.

And what if it was true? In his wildest dreams, in his very *best* dreams, he could fly. And to be able to become *invisible*? That was more than he dared even dream of.

Dave pinched himself, but he was, in fact, not dreaming.

"Hello?" he asked, peering behind the bookcase. "Where'd you go?"

Just as he was beginning to fear that the *lizard* had disappeared, Sticky emerged over the top of a row of books, dragging the ancient Aztec wrist-band behind him.

"Holy smokes!" Dave gasped, for it was plain to see that this was no ordinary bracelet.

It glowed like a band of sunshine.

It shimmered like a deep pool of molten gold.

It had designs on it that were both foreign and mysterious. Designs that seemed to hold the secrets of an entire civilization.

Designs that, without a doubt, held the promise of power.

"Holy smokes!" Dave gasped again.

"So, *señor*," Sticky said, "do you still think I'm a liar?"

Dave's head wagged slowly from side to side.

"Do you want to be able to fly and go invisible? Do you want to be able to lift boulders like pebbles and climb walls with ease? Do you want the speed of a roadrunner and the—"

"Yes," Dave gasped. "Yes!"

Sticky crossed his arms and cocked his head. "Then you must promise this, *señor:* you will tell no one about the wristband, and you will tell no one that I can talk."

"*No* one?" Dave asked, for even in his understandably stunned state of mind, he knew that this would be difficult. He had a talking lizard! And a wristband that (he now believed) could make him *fly*.

How could he *not* tell someone about it?

But despite his understandably stunned state of mind, Dave did manage to realize that if he did tell someone—*anyone*—about any of it, the lizard would probably never speak to him again. And if that happened, who'd believe him?

People would think that he was crazy!

Mad!

Wholly and totally mental!

Or worse, a complete dork.

So with all these thoughts muddling through

his stunned state of mind, Dave grudgingly agreed to Sticky's conditions:

He would never tell a soul about the wristband.

He would never tell a soul that the lizard could talk.

"Very good," Sticky said. "Because if you do, I will never talk to you again, and people will think you're *loco*, man. Or worse, a complete dork."

In the wink of an eye, Sticky had scurried up Dave's leg and onto his shoulder, where he looked Dave directly in the eye and said, "So, *señor*, are you with me?"

Dave nodded.

"You will help me get the power ingots away from that wicked *ratero* Damien Black?"

"I will!" Dave said, his head bobbing with growing enthusiasm. "I swear I will!"

"I have to warn you, *señor*," Sticky said slyly, "it won't be easy. . . ."

"I don't care!" Dave cried. "We're good, he's evil! We can do it! We can!"

Sticky smiled.

They bumped fists.

And so the pact was made.

For weeks after, Sticky and his new partner schemed and plotted and planned, carefully detailing ways to retrieve the power ingots. But in the end, they chucked it all and simply headed for Damien Black's house, armed with the determination to get inside any way they could.

So! Now that you know what Dave and Sticky were doing, creeping through a frightening forest and an oozy, stinky cave toward the underbelly of a nightmarish mansion, let's get back to them, shall we?

They are, after all, in grave peril. . . .

Chapter 4
CRUNCHY, SLOOOOOPY, GROSS, AND GOOPY

The musty passageway in which Dave and Sticky found themselves did indeed lead away from the stench and dangling moss and fluttery bats of the deep, dark cave.

Which was, at first, quite a relief.

Sticky was on Dave's shoulder now, helping him keep an eagle eye out for booby traps.

Or telltale corpses.

Or tripwire daggers hidden in walls.

But they saw nothing. It seemed safe.

Ah, how deceiving cramped, musty passage-ways can be.

"Do you have any idea where this leads?" Dave whispered.

"Thataway," Sticky said, pointing ahead.

Dave frowned at the gecko. "Oh, that's so helpful. Thank you very much."

They proceeded along the passageway until a strange sound in the distance caused Dave to raise a finger and whisper, "Shhhh."

"I wasn't making a peep, *hombre*."

"Shhhh!"

"But I—"

"Shhhhhh!"

Sticky rolled his eyes. "Ay-ay-ay."

"Ay-ay-ay yourself," Dave grumbled. He moved forward, trying to figure out what he was hearing.

It was a watery sound.

A watery, *crunchy* sound.

A watery, crunchy, *slurpy* sound.

No, wait. It was really more *slooooopy* than slurpy.

Yes. That was it. A watery, crunchy, slooooopy sound.

Dave couldn't imagine what made such a sound. He held the torch in front of them as far as he could reach, and at long last he could see . . . something.

But what was it?

"Is that a waterfall?" he asked at last.

"It doesn't look like a regular waterfall to me, *señor*," Sticky replied.

It was, indeed, much too slooooopy and crunchy to be simply water. Yet it fell like water. And it blocked the entire passageway, just as a waterfall would.

As they grew closer, Dave could feel something slooooopy and *goopy* crunching underfoot. He checked his shoe, and when he saw what was stuck in the treads of his sneaker, his face contorted in disbelief. "Snails?" He looked at the slooooopy, crunchy barrier in front of them. "A waterfall of *snails*?"

And yes. That's exactly what it was. A

crunchy, slooooopy, goopy (and, intermittently, poopy) waterfall of snails.

They stood there for a moment, just staring as the watery wall of snails splashed into a wide, deep trough in the dirt before mysteriously draining away.

At last Sticky shook his head and said, "That Señor Black is one *loco* honcho. . . ."

"Crazy doesn't even begin to describe it," Dave muttered.

Dave stuck the bottom end of the torch into the waterfall, creating a small window beneath the torch through which he could look. The path continued on the other side, but there seemed to be no way to reach it

without going through a torrent of snails and water.

Dave withdrew the torch and then just stood facing the waterfall, saying nothing. Finally Sticky said, "Are you planning to stare at it all day, *señor*?"

"Huh?"

"*Ándale, hombre*. Giddyap! Move it!"

"You expect me to go through *that*?"

Sticky tapped his little gecko chin and said, "Hmm. How do I say this . . . ?" He pulled a face at Dave. "*SÍ, SEÑOR!*"

So Dave took a deep breath and charged through the waterfall, leaping over the deep trough.

"Ouch-ouch-ouch!" he cried as he went through, for the experience was much like being hit by an avalanche of slimy rocks.

"*Ouchie-huahua!*" Sticky cried, too, for he hadn't had the sense to hide inside Dave's sweatshirt.

On the other side, Dave shook off slimy water and sloopy snails and revived the sputtering torch. "That is too weird to believe."

The torch now illuminated a fork in the passageway ahead of them. To the left was a cavern, with stalactites jutting down from the ceiling and stalagmites poking up from the floor. There was something foreboding about the cavern. To Dave, it looked like the gaping mouth of a monster. A monster with row upon row of dripping, deadly teeth.

A monster just waiting for something to chew on.

Yet to the right was a blood-red door, covered with dangling shrunken heads. The sort of shrunken heads you think of when you hear the term "witch doctor."

Or "tribal warrior."

Or, quite obviously, "headhunter."

Each head was about the size of an apple, dark

hair intact, eyes and lips sewn closed with coarse lengths of hemp.

These were not plastic toys.

Not pig-hide replicas.

They were real.

Bone-chillingly real.

"Those are *real*," Dave whispered, shivering from a chill that went, as you might have guessed, clear down to his bones.

"Ay-ay-*yowy*," Sticky whispered in return, his little gecko bones rattling inside his little gecko body. And then, as if offering an explanation for why one might have dozens of shrunken heads adorning one's door, he said, "He's a collector."

"Of *heads*? I thought you said he was a treasure hunter!"

Sticky nodded. "To him, these are also treasures. He has them in the house, too. He thinks they bring luck."

Dave raised an eyebrow in Sticky's direction. "Like geckos do?"

"I'm nothing like a shrunken head!" Sticky snapped. Then he muttered, "You cut me to the quick again, *señor*."

"Sorry." Dave looked back at the door. "So if they bring good luck, does that mean that's a lucky door?"

"Are you asking me, or those guys hanging on it?" Sticky asked.

Dave sighed. "Would you help me out here? Which way do you think we should go? How do we get into the *house*?"

So Sticky quit with the muttery remarks, and in the end, they agreed to go through the shrunken-head door. It was, after all, a door, and it's a well-known fact that doors and houses are usually connected.

Unfortunately for Dave, the doorknob was also a shrunken head—something he (quite understandably) did not want to touch. But faced with his other choices (going into a monster-mouthed cavern or giving up), Dave at last grabbed the shrunken-head doorknob and twisted.

The door creaked open.

The shrunken heads clonked and bonked like a hollow-headed door chime. "Ay *caramba!*" Sticky whispered. "You're waking the dead!"

The thought sent shivers down Dave's spine as he stepped through the doorway and into a large, empty room. A large, empty room with no windows but one, two, three, four, five, six, seven, *eight* doors.

The moment they were completely inside, the door they'd just come through slammed closed behind them. (So make that *nine* doors.) Only then did Dave realize that there were no handles (or shrunken-head knobs) on any of the doors.

And worse, it seemed that the clonking, bonking shrunken heads on the outside had indeed awakened a spirit.

An *evil* spirit.

"Wellllcome!" an eerie voice boomed. "So glad you could drop by! I hope you've planned to stay awhile . . . like for the rest of your life! Bwaa-ha-ha-ha-ha!"

Sticky dived inside Dave's sweatshirt, crying, "That's him! It's Damien Black!"

Dave looked around madly, jerking the torch from one side of the room to the other. "Where? I don't see him!"

"He's evil like that!" Sticky called through the fabric of Dave's sweatshirt. "He can be everywhere and nowhere, all at the same time!"

Dave's heart was pounding.

His eyelids were peeled way back.

Again he spun in a circle, searching for the dastardly treasure hunter, but all he saw were nine doors.

Nine doors and no way out.

Chapter 5
THE ONE WAY OUT

"Bwaa-ha-ha-ha-ha" came the villainous voice again. "Bwaa-ha-ha-ha-ha . . . ha-ha . . . ha-ha . . . ha-ha . . ."

Dave quit spinning in circles. "Wait a minute! That's just a recording! And it's *stuck*."

It was then that he finally noticed a cheesy little speaker mounted to the ceiling. A ceiling that was made of giant dangling boulders. "It's just a cheesy little speaker!" he cried, jabbing it with the end of the torch until it quit ha-ha-ha'ing at them.

Dave searched the bouldery ceiling for other hidden devices. Like surveillance eyes. Or movement sensors. Or laser beam alarms. But he searched in vain, for you see, Damien Black did not believe in the use of modern technology. He believed in the use of clever, sneaky things: disguises and booby traps and cheesy little speakers; secret rooms and hidden poisons and scary, flappy beasts.

And, oh yes, he also believed in agonizing deaths in dungeons and torture chambers.

He was, in short, an old-fashioned, truly demented villain.

And Dave and Sticky were, in fact, quite stuck in one of his demented little rooms with dangling boulders and knobless doors.

Dave tried prying at each and every door.

Tried pushing on each and every door.

Tried *pounding* on each and every door.

It wasn't until Dave lost his temper and *kicked* one that he discovered a way out.

Whoosh, the door swept inward, and *clonk*, the top swung down, clobbering him on the head.

"Ouch!" Dave cried.

"*Ouchie-huahua*," Sticky cried, although he hadn't actually been hit by the swinging, clonking door.

Dave scrambled backward as the door creaked on its peg like a giant teeter-totter. No monster came into the room. No voices bwaa-ha-ha'd. Not even a bat fluttered.

So Dave crept forward, holding the torch well ahead of him so he could see what lay beyond the plank of wagging wood.

"An elevator?" he whispered.

"Freaky *frijoles*! Are you serious, man?" Sticky pushed forward to get a better look. "He always dashed me up and down stairs. Twisty, curvy, creaky stairs! With no handrails. And all this time he had an *elevator*?"

"Uh, maybe not," Dave said, moving in closer. "I think it's just *painted* like an elevator."

He was exactly right. From the buttons on the

wall to the floor numbers above the door, the room was painted so meticulously that as Dave entered it, he still didn't quite believe he was not in an elevator. Except for one small detail:

There was a giant tongue of a door sticking out at them.

"I don't get it," Dave said. He looked up into the vast, dark shaft above them, as there was no ceiling to this strange elevator room either. "Why paint a room like an elevator if it doesn't move?"

"Hmm," Sticky said, tapping his chin thoughtfully. "Maybe that's just what you do when you're a chimmy-chunga, binga-bunga, *loco*-berry burrito?"

"Nobody's *this* crazy," Dave murmured. He looked around at the teeter-totter door, the long shaft up, the elevator walls, the dangling boulders outside. . . . Then suddenly he put them all together in his mind and cried, "It's a catapult!"

Sticky dived for the safety of Dave's sweatshirt. "A cat-a-who? Where?"

Dave stepped onto the door like one might step onto the end of a teeter-totter. "Not a cat, a catapult! It shoots you into the air."

"*Asombrrrrroso!*" Sticky said, scrambling out from inside Dave's sweatshirt. But then it struck his little gecko brain that perhaps this was not so awesome after all.

Perhaps this was dangerous.

(Perhaps, indeed!)

"Uh, *señor?*" Sticky asked. "How does it shoot us? Where do we go? Will we get smashed like pimply papayas?"

Dave turned to face him. "Like pimply papayas?"

"I'm really just talking about you, *señor*, not me." Sticky shrugged. "I don't have pimples. And I could just crawl up."

Dave shook his head. "Thanks a lot." He went back to searching for a lever. Or a switch. Or a hoist. Or some thingamajig that would shoot them up the shaft.

All he could find, though, was a painted button that said UP, and who in his right mind pushes a painted button and expects it to *do* anything?

"Why don't you push the UP button, *señor?*"

Dave's head snapped to face Sticky, for into his mind had popped the same question that has undoubtedly popped into yours: "You can *read?*" He squinted at the gecko. "Who taught you to read?"

Sticky shrugged. "You pick things up in life, *señor.* Now push it. See what happens."

"Nothing's gonna happen. It's paint!"

"Whatever you say," Sticky said, and then lickety-split, he scurried across Dave's shoulders and down his arm, spun in the air, and slammed the UP button with his tail.

It was fortunate that Sticky's little kung-fu maneuver landed him back on Dave's sleeve, because outside, a boulder came crashing down, instantly catapulting them skyward.

"Hurling *habañerooooooos!*" Sticky cried, his voice echoing off the walls of the shaft as they flew up, up, up.

The shaft was painted the whole way up. They blasted by the image of an eerie night sky with a giant moon, bats, and wispy clouds. They flew past

screaming ghosts, and ghouls from the grave. And then, just as they were losing momentum, they found themselves approaching the most frightening sight of all.

A man with black hair.

Pale skin.

A twisty mustache, devilish smile, and glinting black eyes.

His coat was long and black and flowing behind him.

His boots were black, too, with bent and tarnished silver buckles. And the axe he carried was as tall as he was, and at least as fiendish. It had cracks and nicks in the edges of its double blade, yet it glistened evilly. Like it, too, had a dastardly past.

"Creeping creosote!" Sticky gasped. "It's him!"

As real as it looked, it was merely a painting of Damien Black standing on the edge of a cliff alongside a jagged wooden sign that read:

DANGER
DO NOT
ENTER

Dave knew the man on the wall was just paint, but it crossed his mind that painted objects in this shaft were sometimes more than merely paint. What might happen if he touched him?

At that very moment, he came face to face with Damien Black's glinting painted eyes and decided that touching him was not a good idea.

Not a good idea at all.

It was, however, also at that very moment that Dave stopped going up and started tumbling down. You see, even in strangely painted catapulting shafts, gravity still rules the day. What goes up will most definitely come down.

That is, unless something stops it.

"Aaaah!" Dave cried, looking around madly for something to stop him. "Aaaah!"

It was at this point that Sticky leapt from

Dave's sleeve, climbed lickety-split up the wall, and slapped the ENTER part of the painted DO NOT ENTER sign.

Kafffffflank! A plank shot out beneath Dave, and *brrrr-wack-yak-yak-yak-yak*, a section of the shaft wall went up like a rolltop desk.

Sticky scurried down the wall and reunited with Dave, who was futilely scrabbling for his dropped torch as the plank beneath him began to retract, pulling him into the opening in the wall. It was as though the shaft had opened its mouth and stuck out its tongue, much as a frog would catch a fly.

Moments later, they were inside, not a frog, but a room. A *normal* room, with four walls, a window, furniture, and a rug.

And there was no Damien Black in sight.

"We made it!" Dave whispered, looking out the window at the forest beneath them. "We're inside the house!"

They sneaky-toed over to the door, which had

a normal doorknob. (It was bent and dented, but it was metal, at least, and not somebody's head.)

Dave eeeeeased the door open.

They peeeeeeeked outside.

And of all the dastardly, dangerous, daggery things that might have been there, you will never, I promise you, *never* guess what awaited them on the other side of the door.

Chapter 6
CONFUSING, CONFOUNDING, AND JUST PLAIN CREEPY

"A burro?" Dave gasped. "In a *house*?"

But, of course, this was no ordinary house, and, as it turns out, this was no ordinary burro.

"*Ay caramba!*" Sticky gasped. "What is she doing here?"

"Good question," Dave replied, not fully grasping the significance of Sticky's question *or* the *ay caramba!*

You see, there are *ay carambas*, and then there are *ay caRAMbas*. In Stickynese, they can mean anything from "oh brother" to "oh wow" to "the world is about to explode!"

And this particular *ay caramba* was, without a doubt, an *ay caRAMba ay caramba*.

53

In other words, this burro was very bad news.

"No, *amigo*! You don't understand!" Sticky whispered frantically. "That's Rosie!"

"You know this burro? Is she mean? Can she talk?"

"Talk? No! She's dumb as donkey dung!"

"So what's the problem?"

"The problem, *señor*, is that she belongs to the Bandito Brothers!" He slapped his little gecko forehead. "Ay-ay-ay. I can't believe they're here."

"Wait. Who are the Bandito Brothers?"

Sticky looked everywhere but at Dave.

"Stickyyyyy . . ."

"All right, all right." Sticky puffed out his little gecko chest in an attempt to stand tall. "I used to live with them, okay? Before I joined that back-stabbing treasure hunter."

"You lived with banditos? *Bandits?*"

"*Sí, señor,*" Sticky said with a shrug. "What can I say? They accepted me."

Dave, who is no fool, put the pieces together lickety-split. "They accepted you because you had sticky fingers and would steal things for them?"

Again, Sticky gave a little shrug. "Before me, they were poor as dirt. After me? They were loaded." He looked out at the burro, who was chewing over an enormous pile of thistly, thorny weeds. "Those *bobos* banditos have teamed up with that *ratero* Black? I can't believe it."

Dave's face contorted in the way that only a very unhappy face can contort. "So we're not dealing with just an evil, demented treasure hunter here? We're also dealing with *bobos* banditos? How many?"

"Well," said Sticky, counting them off on his fingers, "there's Tito—he's big like an ox with a head full of rocks. There's Pablo—he looks like a rat and stinks like a bat. And then there's Angelo—he's scar-faced and scary and ugly and hairy."

"I don't care what they look like! How many are there? Three?"

"Oh, you care, *señor*. And *sí*. *Tres*."

"Are you sure they're here?"

Sticky shrugged. "Why else would Rosie be here? She's their transportation."

Dave's face was now screwed around so far that one eye was almost covered by a cheek, and his mouth was twisted nearly to his ear. "Their transportation? The three of them ride one burro?"

Again, Sticky shrugged. "It's a tight fit."

"But . . . how do you know that's *their* burro? It could be a different donkey . . . couldn't it?"

At that moment, Rosie stopped feasting from her thistly, thorny mountain of weeds and turned to look at them. Her lips pushed forward, revealing a single, yellowed, bucked front tooth in the middle of her weed-filled mouth.

"It's Rosie," Sticky said, for there was no denying the dental details.

At that moment, Dave considered turning back, which I'm sure you'll agree was a prudent thing to consider. After all, he no longer had just the one dangerously demented villain to outwit. He now had three additional foes. And a bucktoothed burro to boot.

But then Dave envisioned the return route out of the mansion: down the shaft (who knows how), into the knobless room (and who knows how they'd get out of *that*), through the waterfall of goopy, sloopy snails, down a musty passageway (with no torch to light the way), through the oozy, stinky cave of fluttery bats, and finally out through the dark and dangerous forest to squeeze through the gate.

In the end, Dave decided that going forward would be safer. After all, Damien Black would not enter his house in such a bizarre manner. Surely there was a door somewhere. A simple door with normal knobs that led away from this maniacal mansion.

Poor Dave. He still had so much to learn.

"So now what?" he asked at last.

"So now we find the dungeon," Sticky replied.

Ah, yes. The dungeon. Sticky had told Dave that the dungeon was where the power ingots were kept. Power ingots, which, if you'll recall, were why these two had endured bats and tunnels and snails and shrunken heads and catapulting shafts in the first place.

To his credit, Sticky had warned Dave that the dungeon housed a ferocious dragon. Not the fire-breathing sort found in made-up fairy tales. A *real* dragon, found in real-life stories, such as this one.

A dragon with dark, scaly skin.

Big eyes.

Sprawling legs and sharp claws.

A three-hundred-pound dragon with a tail as long as his body and a long, yellow, forked tongue.

A cold-blooded, meat-eating beast.

One that could kill with a single bite of his disease-ridden, bacteria-breeding mouth.

Dave had been undaunted. "A Komodo dragon? Those are just oversized lizards!"

"Ay-ay-ay," Sticky had murmured, for it was clear that Dave had no idea what he was getting into.

But whose fault was that?

He would simply have to pay the price for being an all-knowing thirteen-year-old boy.

So Dave and his sticky-footed friend stepped through the doorway and entered the room that Rosie was in.

I use the word "room" loosely here, as this was more a large, six-sided intersection of hallways than an actual room. There were walls (and a ceiling) and an actual door across from the door they'd just come through, but there were also four shadowy passageways leading to (or from) this intersecting room.

Dave looked around at his choices and whispered, "Which way?"

"Uh . . . thataway!" Sticky said, pointing with great conviction to a hallway on the left.

So Dave went past the bucktoothed burro and sneaky-toed down the hallway that Sticky had pointed to. But after a few minutes he whispered, "Does any of this look familiar?"

"*Sí, señor,*" Sticky lied. "We turn right, right here."

They were soon meandering through a dingy, dusty, cobwebby maze of hallways.

It was a labyrinth of passageways.

A confounding collection of creepy corridors.

And after many twists and turns and sneaky-toeing along with Sticky pointing the way, they found themselves face to face with . . . a bucktoothed burro.

"No!" Dave cried. He glared at Sticky. "You have no idea where we are, do you?"

Sticky looked away. "It's a big house, *señor.*"

"So what are we supposed to do?"

Sticky shrugged. "Try again?"

So off they went again, through the confounding

collection of creepy corridors. Only this time Dave went where *he* thought they should go.

And, as you may already have guessed, they wound up face to face with . . . a bucktoothed burro.

"No!" Dave cried again.

This time, however, they heard an evil, hissy voice coming from down a hallway.

But which hallway?

"It's him! It's him for real! Quick, *señor*, hide!" Sticky whispered.

Now, it's a well-known fact that when panic strikes, the logic receptors in your brain stop working. They just freeze up, leaving logical thoughts out in the cold and forcing you to do whatever comes to mind, regardless of how ridiculous or irrational it is.

In Dave's case, panic had most definitely struck, and the only place he could think to hide was in Rosie's thistly, thorny mountain of weeds.

So he dived in and covered himself quickly, then made a peephole through the weeds.

Sticky did the same.

They both held their breath.

They stayed stick-still.

Then in walked the villain himself.

The dastardly, demented Damien Black.

Chapter 7
THE DASTARDLY, DEMENTED DAMIEN BLACK

Damien Black was taller than Dave expected. Perhaps that was because he was looking up at him from among thistly, thorny weeds on the ground, but nonetheless, he seemed both taller and oilier than Dave expected.

By oily I do not mean deep-fried.

By oily I mean slick.

Slippery.

Shifty in a way that only dastardly, demer
villains know how to be.

And although he was talking, it was r
himself, as dastardly, demented villains are
to do. Oh no. He was talking to the
Brothers. Two of them, that is. The third

(the one who was big like an ox and had a head full of rocks), was in a cell in the dungeon, tied up and awaiting his fate as dragon dinner should his brothers fail to satisfy Damien's demands.

"It must be him," Damien was saying. "And he's probably with some fool who thinks he can rob me. That annoying lizard doesn't know how to keep his mouth shut! Yakety-yakety-yak, all the time. If there's one thing I can't stand, it's yakety-yakking."

For some reason, this caused the two Bandito Brothers to begin yakking:

"But that's a good thing, right, Mr. Black?"

"How else would you ever find him?"

"He's little!"

"Just a lizard!"

Through the weeds, Dave watched the two Bandito Brothers trail behind Damien Black. He was now glad Sticky had told him that Pablo looked like a rat and smelled like a bat (not that

he could smell him through the musty, thorny, thistly weeds, but he *could* see that he was small-boned with a pointy nose and a scraggly mustache) and that Angelo was scar-faced and scary and ugly and hairy (although the hair was not so much on his head as it was on his arms—a fact Dave couldn't ignore, as Angelo was wearing a dingy oversized shirt with the sleeves ripped out).

What Sticky had neglected to tell him was that the brothers also wore bandoliers of ammunition crisscrossing their chests. And that their boots had spurs. And that their teeth were capped here and there in gold.

"Shut up, you fools!" Mr. Black commanded. "If that lizard is here on his own, why do I need you?"

"To catch him?"

"Yes, Mr. Black. To catch him!"

"We're the only other ones who know what he looks like!"

"And he does not know we are working with you!"

Damien Black stopped dead in his tracks and turned to face them. "You are *not* working with me. You are doing as I say so your brother doesn't die a slow, agonizing death!"

"He's not really our brother!"

"And we keep telling you—we would do what you say anyway!"

"Why do you think we followed you here?"

"We hate that lousy lizard."

"He's creepy!"

"He's sneaky!"

"He cheated us!"

"Betrayed us!"

"Double-crossed us!"

"Duped us!"

"So we're happy to help you, Mr. Black."

"Very happy."

Hearing this made steam shoot out of Sticky's

ears. (Not that it actually *was*, it just felt that way to the lizard.) He wanted to push through the weeds and shout, "You rotten *rateros*! *You* betrayed *me*." But he was so mad, so incredibly mad, that he held stick-still and vowed on his little gecko life that he would strip Damien Black and those *bobos* banditos of the power ingots. He would get them, and through Dave, he would then get his revenge! Indeed, he would!

Dave, on the other hand, did not like what he'd heard. Was *he* being duped? Was Sticky playing him for a fool? Was he risking life and limb for a sneaky, creepy, dirty, double-crossing cheater?

But Damien Black was moving again. Moving and talking. "My alarm went off. Somebody came up the chute. No one would dare enter unless they knew what I had."

"What *do* you have, Mr. Black?"

"Yes, Mr. Black. What are we looking for?"

"A lizard!" Damien shouted. "A lizard and anyone he's with!" He glared at them. "And if you insist on knowing more, I'll have to kill you."

"Oooh," they both said, taking a step back. Then Pablo's face twitched nervously as he asked, "But . . . after you have what you want, can we have the lizard?"

Damien's eyes pinched into devilish slits, but then he thought better of telling the brothers the truth. In other words, he decided to lie. "Yes," he said. "But not until after I have retrieved the item he stole from me."

Now, the alarm to which Damien Black had referred was not a clangy alarm like one might find at a firehouse.

Or a buzzy alarm like one might hear when entering a secured area.

Or even a honky alarm that one might hear if a power plant were about to explode.

No, this was a tinkly alarm. A tinkly-winkly

alarm. The sort of alarm one might find on, say, the collar of a cat.

It was, in short, a bell.

A single tinkly-winkly bell.

When Dave and Sticky had entered the house, that single tinkly-winkly bell had been activated, and the sound had tinkly-winkled along echoing tubes throughout the entire house.

But was it an intruder? Or merely another bat, setting off the alarm? This was something Damien Black did not know. Once inside the next room, however, Damien got his answer.

An intruder was afoot!

You see, Damien Black may not have believed in modern technology, but he made full use of dusting powder. Flour, actually. He kept a fine sprinkling of it on the floor by the catapult doorway, and there, before his devilish eye-slits, were footprints.

Sneaky sneaker footprints.

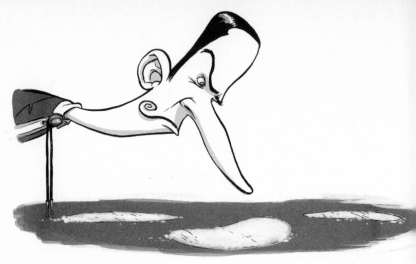

Size, oh, maybe ten.

"To the dungeon!" he shouted, then whooshed back through the oversized intersection, past Rosie and the heaping pile of thistly, thorny weeds (and intruders), and down the hallway.

"To the dungeon!" Sticky cried the moment the villain and the two Bandito Brothers were gone.

Dave stood and shook off the weeds.

He sneaky-peeked down the hallway where Damien Black had gone.

Then off they went.

To the dungeon!

Chapter 8
THE DUNGEON

The hard part wasn't following Damien Black and the Bandito Brothers. The hard part was not being seen.

"Too bad we don't have the Invisibility ingot, eh, *señor?*" Sticky whispered as they ducked back for the third time. "This would be eeeeeasysneezy."

"But we don't, all right? Now shh!"

"But when we get it, all you do is click it into the wristband, and *poof,* we're gone."

"We? You'll disappear, too?"

"If I'm holding on to you, *hombre.*" Sticky gave a little gecko snicker. "And believe me, I will be!"

The thought of this kept Dave going. Invisibility would be cooler than cool. It would be, in Stickynese, *asombroso*.

And flying. He just *had* to get his hands on that flying ingot. No more trudging up seven flights to get to the apartment. No more riding his bike or fixing flat tires—he'd just turn invisible and fly everywhere!

But then he remembered: the powers only worked one at a time.

Aw, who cared? He'd figure something out. The point was, he'd be able to *fly*.

"You didn't lose the powerband, did you?" Sticky was asking.

Dave held back while Damien and the Brothers went through a tall, narrow door down the hallway. "Are you kidding?" He could feel it on his arm, heavy and warm. Perhaps it had been a wristband to a powerful Aztec warrior, but on Dave it was an armband. "It's not going anywhere!"

"I hope not, *señor*," Sticky muttered. "Because if you lose it, *we're* not going anywhere."

"Just get us to the power ingots, all right? Leave the rest to me."

So they waited until they thought the coast must be clear, then eased open the tall, narrow door and sneaky-peeked inside.

No Damien.

No Brothers.

No other doorways.

Just maps.

Maps *everywhere*.

"I know where we are!" Sticky cried. Then, as if sharing a dark and spicy secret, he whispered, "This is the map room!"

Dave rolled his eyes. "And how do we get through the map room to . . . to wherever that madman has gone?"

"Thataway!" Sticky said, pointing to the floor.

Sure enough, beneath the rug was a trapdoor.

A trapdoor that, Dave discovered, led to steep, crooked, spiraling steps that led, well, down.

No, not just down.

Down, down, *down*.

As they descended into the deep darkness, they could hear Damien's voice echoing through the . . . down-ness.

Dave whispered, "Does this take us to the dungeon?"

"*Sí, señor!*" Then he asked, "Can't you *see, señor*? You're stumbling around like you're blind!"

"It's dark in here!"

For a gecko like Sticky, there was plenty of light to see by. He yanked on Dave's ear and said, "Theeees way! You're going to fall off if you don't watch it!"

"Fall off?"

"*Sí!*" He kept tugging. "Come over this way. Hug the wall. And watch out for rats! They're as big as cats and they're everywhere!"

Some-
thing as big
as a cat scurried
across Dave's feet.
Dave did a little
dance, nearly lost his
balance, then said, "This
place is a nightmare!"

"Ay *chihuahua*, don't I
know?"

The place was, in fact, worse than a nightmare. Perhaps one could dream of tall, oozy, slimy
walls and creaky, crooked steps or of rats scurrying
and bats fluttering, cobwebs snagging and spiders
dangling . . . but the smell . . . oh, the smell! Who
could dream a smell like that?

No, they were definitely wide awake, and the

farther down they went, the stronger the stench became until it was nose-pinching, eye-stinging *awful*.

"What *is* that smell?" Dave whispered, his eyes at last adjusting to the darkness.

"Death," Sticky explained, his voice small and shivery. "We're getting near the dragon pit."

A few steps later, Dave came to a stop. "I feel like we're walking into a trap."

The reason he sensed this was because of something even creepier than the smell or the oozy, slimy walls or the scurrying rats and fluttering bats and dreadful, dangling spiders.

He had just noticed the silence.

The sudden, eerie silence.

"The voices have stopped," Dave whispered ever so softly.

Sticky tugged on Dave's ear, leading him off the spiraling stairs and into an uneven crevice in the wall. It was barely wide enough for Dave to hide in, and the cold, damp walls were giving him the chilly-willies. He wanted out. He wanted out badly.

But then he heard footsteps approaching.

"Do not move a muscle," Sticky whispered into Dave's ear.

Dave held his breath as a dark figure in black boots and a caped coat crept up the stairs.

Crept past them.

Dave kept holding his breath.

For another minute.

Maybe two.

Then the nose-pinching air was shattered by an ear-splitting squeal.

"Blasted varmint!" Damien shouted, and then a pitiful *screeeeeeeeeeeech* descended into the dungeon until finally there was a *thump*.

And then, from somewhere beneath them, came the sound of muffled machine-gun fire.

Only it wasn't a machine gun.

Or even a six-shooter.

It was the dragon, charging his prey.

"It was only rats!" Damien called down the stairs at the Bandito Brothers. Then he laughed his evil, demented laugh. "Bwaa-ha-ha-ha-ha! Hors d'oeuvres for my pet!"

The black boots and caped coat strode by again, faster on their way down than they'd been on their way up. "And if you don't want your brother to wind up as the main course," he called down the stairs, "you'll do everything I say!"

"He's not really our brother!" Angelo called.

"Do I care, you fool?" Damien shouted back.

After Damien was gone, the coast was clear. Dave stayed in the narrow crevice longer than was necessary. He had heard the cat-sized rat fall to its doom. He had heard the rapid fire of the Komodo dragon's claws. He was, it's fair to say, scared.

What had he gotten himself into?

Was flying really worth *this*?

"*Ándale, hombre!*" Sticky urged. "If he moves the power ingots, we'll never find them."

But Dave stayed put, and through chattering teeth, he whispered, "Why would he bring the Burrito Brothers down here? It doesn't make sense."

Sticky rolled his eyes. "Not *Burrito*, Bandito. They're a mariachi band, okay? It has nothing to do with food. And they're not really brothers. That's the name of their band."

This was just what Dave needed to get his mind off of rats and dragons and death. "*What?* You said they were bandits! Now they're a *band*? Are you lying about *everything*? Are you just out to get me killed?"

"Ay-ay-ay." Sticky rolled his eyes. "Look, the Bandito Brothers were a band, but people stopped hiring them because they were awful and they'd steal stuff from parties. So they became the *outlaw* Bandito Brothers." Sticky shrugged. "Stealing is easier than playing."

"What about those bandoliers?" Dave asked. "Are they real? Why are they still wearing them?"

Again, Sticky shrugged. "It's part of their costume, *señor*. Without six-shooters, you have nothing to fear." Then he added, "Tito uses his as suspenders."

Dave shook his head, remembering his original question. "But why did Damien bring the Bandito Brothers down here?"

"The same reason he always dragged me down here—to make them fear him and his dragon." Sticky frowned. "He is training them."

This conversation had somehow calmed Dave enough to continue down the steps toward the dungeon. He hugged the oozy, slimy wall closely, approaching a lighted area beneath them. Soon a huge pit came into view. The floor of the pit was mostly sand, and the sides curved out and then in again like a fishbowl. Across the pit from Dave was the dragon's den—a deep, shadowy cave that gashed through the otherwise smooth wall. And in the center of the pit was a tree that wasn't quite a tree—it was more a trunk with branches but with no leaves.

"There it is!" Sticky whispered, pointing to the ugliest beast Dave had ever seen. It seemed like a creature from another world. Another time. Another *dimension*. A hungry creature with a lumbering gait and a long, flicking forked tongue. A vile creature that stank of death and decay and, oh yes, disgusting dragon doo-doo.

"Hello, my sweet!" Damien Black called to it from the rim of the pit. He went out of view for a moment, then suddenly the treasure hunter was *in* the pit, holding an enormous goose by the neck. "Here you are!" he cooed at the dragon, then flung the goose across the sand and sauntered toward the dragon's den.

The goose flapped and honked, manically, trying to get away from the dragon, but the beast was

hungry, fast, and ferocious, and there was no escaping him.

"Do not think that will work for you," Sticky whispered. "That evil *hombre* is putting on a show for the Brothers." He tugged Dave by the ear, turning him so they were eye to eye. "Stay here. Do not go into the pit. The dragon will kill you."

And with that, Sticky jumped off Dave's shoulder and scurried into the pit.

Chapter 9
THE PIT OF DOOM

A Komodo dragon senses its prey with its foot-long tongue. It can hear (although not very well) and can see (although what it recognizes, primarily, is movement), but it is the long yellow tongue that tells it the most. Each tip of the forked tongue delivers airborne molecules from potential prey to organs on the roof of its mouth. Organs that can tell, amazingly, if the left tip has more prey molecules than the right tip. Organs that let the dragon know which way to go.

This is why the Komodo dragon's tongue flicks in and out so frequently.

This is why the tongue is forked.

This is why the dragon's head swings from left to right as it walks.

It is looking for something to kill.

Komodo dragons typically like big prey. Prey that will sustain them for days on end. Prey like deer and boars and goats, and yes, when available, humans.

And, like a hinge-jawed garbage disposal, the Komodo dragon will consume nearly all of its prey with its large, serrated teeth. From brain to bones, it leaves very little of its victim behind.

A Komodo dragon does *not*, however, usually bother with little things like mice or toads or speedy gecko lizards. There's not enough there worth hunting.

So it was with a certain amount of immunity that Sticky now entered the dragon's pit and scurried across it toward the den.

Dave, as you might imagine, knew none of this. All he knew was that he'd risked life and limb to transport a sneaky, talking gecko lizard into a devil-ish dungeon, where he was now totally alone.

Well, alone in the sense that he had no one to talk to.

There were still, of course, the Bandito Brothers.

And where, you ask, were they?

A very good question, and precisely the one Dave was asking himself at that very moment.

To get the answer, Dave crept along, keeping one eye on the dragon's den into which Sticky had disappeared, one on the dragon chomping fe-rociously on his feathered prey, and one on the end of the wall ahead of him, wondering what awaited him around the corner.

(Yes, that would indeed give him three eyes, but under such circumstances, eyes are allowed to dart back and forth doing double duty, so stop counting.)

What Dave discovered was that all three

Bandito Brothers were hanging in separate cages from telescoping cranes. At the moment, the cranes were retracted, but they had the ability to extend out and over the dragon pit and whoosh open, dropping whatever was inside them into the pit.

Now, being fairly new to the ways of sneaky-peeking around disgusting, devilish dungeons, Dave made the mistake of jerking back when he saw the Brothers. Jerking back is the thing one naturally does when trying not to be seen, but it is also, unfortunately, what usually gives one away.

"Did you see that?" Angelo said.

"It was a boy!" Pablo replied.

"Where? Where?" the rocky-brained Tito asked.

"Shhh!" the other two commanded.

Then Pablo said, "Pssst! Boy! We saw you. Now come quickly! Before that insane Mr. Black returns."

"If you help us, we'll help you!" Angelo whispered hoarsely.

"Don't be afraid," Pablo coaxed. "Set us free and we won't tell him you're here." Then, in a sly voice, he added, "And if you don't, we will!"

Had Dave known the Bandito Brothers, he would have expected this. You see, blackmail was a big part of their repertoire.

It was a tactic that they used regularly.

Liberally.

And, as you might suspect, with great relish.

Which is to say, they enjoyed using it as much as one might enjoy using mustard or ketchup or chopped pickles on one's hot dog, as opposed to eating it, say, plain.

Yes, blackmail, the Bandito Brothers all agreed, made everything so much yummier.

But to Dave, the thought of setting the Brothers free did make sense. How could they possibly be on the side of a madman who caged them and threatened them? Surely he could get them to help him recover the power ingots. Or at least escape.

Sticky, had he been there, would most certainly have said, "Freaky *frijoles*! Are you crazy?" or perhaps "Are you a *loco bobo*?" or "Chony baloney, don't free those *rata-tonies*!" or simply "Hello? *Señor Estúpido*?"

But Sticky was not there. Sticky was deep in the dragon's den, sneaking up the cape of Damien's coat as the villain unearthed his most precious treasures and removed the little satchel of power ingots from among old gold coins, exquisite jewels, diamonds, and his favorite loot of all—tiger-eyes. (The stone, not the real thing. Although, with Damien Black, it is understandably confusing.)

So, without Sticky to guide him, Dave decided: he would free the Brothers.

But first, he thought, he should take a step of caution. He needed something to conceal him— to make him not so easily recognized or identified.

But what disguise does a thirteen-year-old boy keep in his backpack? Sticky hadn't slipped one in alongside the matches or the grapes, which just goes to show you how shortsighted a klepto-maniacal lizard can be.

But what *was* in the backpack was his favorite ball cap. A dark red one with a diamondback snake design.

He pulled it on, keeping the bill down as low as possible to cover his face. It wasn't much of a disguise, but at least it was something.

When the Bandito Brothers saw Dave round the corner again, they practically rubbed their hands in glee. In a moment, they would be free! In a moment, they would race across the pit, overpower the madman, and discover what riches he had stored in that dragon's den.

It would indeed be a glorious day in their lives.

"Hurry, friend!" Angelo whispered. "There is no time to lose!"

"Me first!" Tito cried. "Me first!"

"Hush, Tito!" Pablo commanded, then turned to Dave. "Cool hat, dude. Now get busy!"

"How?" Dave asked, for there were big buttons, switches, and levers beside each crane.

"The levers!" Angelo said. "Pull the levers!"

So Dave did.

Thump went Tito as the bottom opened up.

Thump went Pablo.

And, finally, *thump* went Angelo.

"Thank you, friend, thank you!" Angelo said. And then, with a wicked, backstabbing, double-crossing look on his scary, scarry face, he pushed a button on the wall.

A trapdoor beneath Dave's feet fell open.

Whoosh, Dave slid down a slippery metal tube and landed in the sandpit.

And before he could even stand, the flicking tongue of the Komodo dragon was coming his way.

Chapter 10
DOOMED!

"Nice dragon. Good dragon," Dave said as the wagging head and flicking tongue came closer.

Now, it wasn't that the dragon was consciously bad or mean. He was just hungry. The cat-sized rat hadn't filled the void in his stomach. Neither had the goose, which had been more feathers than meat. He was tired of snacks. He wanted a *meal*.

Dave tried to re-enter the tube he'd slid down, but it was far too slick to climb. He looked around madly. The walls of the pit curved inward—he couldn't climb those! The barren tree in the center of the pit had no pegs or branches that he could reach. And it was scarred with deep claw marks. Even if he could climb it, so could the dragon!

There seemed to be no way out.

No dangling ropes.

No catapults.

No elevators (painted or otherwise).

Dave backed along the wall, his heart pounding as the dragon lumbered closer. Flick, flick, flick went the dragon's long tongue. Flick, flick, flick.

Then suddenly *ka-thump*, *ka-thump*, *ka-THUMP* the Bandito Brothers came tumbling out of the slippery tube and into the pit.

Now, I'm sure you're wondering why these three men would willingly slide into the Komodo dragon's killing arena, and I'm afraid it can only be explained this way:

They were, indeed, *bobos* banditos.

Idiotas!

Estúpidos!

You see, to the Bandito Brothers, it did not seem like such a risk.

It seemed wise.

Wily.

Smart!

After all, the dragon was occupied with the boy. All they had to do was sneak around them and overpower Damien Black in the den.

For fearsome bandits such as themselves, it would be easy!

And their plan might actually have worked, except for one thing:

They stank!

Especially Pablo.

You see, to a Komodo dragon, stinky means yummy. And the sudden presence of the Bandito Brothers caused the dragon's foot-long, forked, and yellow tongue great confusion. Ahead of him was dinner, but to the side of him? Wow, did that smell good!

"Uh-oh," Pablo said as the dragon changed direction.

"Not good," Angelo agreed.

"Whoa! He's cool!" Tito giggled, taking a step toward the dragon.

"You idiot!" Angelo said, grabbing him.

But Pablo nudged Angelo and gave him a little signal that meant, Let the dragon have him.

Ah, what a coldhearted, backstabbing, double-crossing, rat-faced bandito he was.

Meanwhile, Dave was hatching a plan of his own. He stood with his back flat against the wall by the den's opening and shouted, "Angelo! Hurry up! We must kill Mr. Black and feed him to the dragon!" Then he changed his voice and called, "I'm coming, Pablo! I'm coming!"

"Huh?" Angelo said, staring at Dave.

"He knows our names?" Pablo gasped. "How does he know our names?"

And then *whoosh*, out of the dragon's den came Damien Black. "You!" he said, his dark and dangerous eyes drilling into the Bandito Brothers. "How did you get away?"

Angelo and Pablo pointed to the place where Dave had been standing, but Dave was no longer there. The instant Damien Black had whooshed out of the den, Dave had whooshed *into* the den.

And that's where he now was, whispering hoarsely, "Sticky? Sticky, where are you?"

But Sticky was no longer in the dragon's den. He was in Damien's coat pocket trying frantically to lift the satchel of power ingots that Damien had removed from the treasure chest in the den. He strained and heaved mightily. If he could just get the bag . . . up. If he could just get it . . . out. . . .

But then he realized that something was terribly wrong. Damien was moving fast. Shouting. Whooshing all over the place!

He stuck his little gecko head up and couldn't help gasping *"Ay caramba!"* when he saw the chaos in the pit. The dragon was stalking Tito. Damien was chasing Pablo and Angelo.

Sticky looked around quickly.

Where was Dave?

He let out a little breath of relief—at least he wasn't in the pit.

But then he saw him, standing in the shadows of the dragon's den.

Ay-ay-ay. Why didn't humans ever listen?

But what could be done now? They were both in the pit and they had to get out. So Sticky waved with one hand. He waved with two. He tried desperately to get Dave's attention as Damien whooshed around the pit.

When Dave did at last see him, the boy could not believe his eyes.

Why was Sticky in that madman's pocket?

Had he switched back over to the demented side?

Was he waving *Adiós*, sucker?

Then Sticky disappeared into the coat pocket, and with a mighty gecko groan, he lifted the satchel of power ingots high enough for Dave to see.

In a flash of understanding, Dave pointed to his arm where the powerband was clamped and looked at Sticky questioningly.

Sticky's head bobbed up and down, and his meaning was clear: *SÍ, SEÑOR!* Why else would I be whooshing around a dragon pit in a madman's pocket?

Dave laughed with relief, but the relief was short-lived.

What was he supposed to do now?

Perhaps an older, wiser person would have been able to stand back in the shadows of a dragon's den and watch the frenetic scene in the pit play out, but Sticky had chosen a thirteen-year-old boy.

Older and wiser were not part of the deal.

So when Dave saw that Sticky was just about to tumble over the edge of the pocket with the satchel of power ingots, he didn't stand in the shadows and watch.

He *charged*.

Sticky saw him coming and choked out "No, *señor!*" as he clonked onto the sand. If Dave had just waited, he would have dragged the satchel to Dave while the dragon and Damien and those *bobos* Bandito Brothers all killed each other.

But Dave wasn't the only one to make a mistake. Sticky had made one, too.

He had spoken.

Now, in your life you will hear many voices, and you will forget nearly all of them. But if you ever hear the voice of a talking gecko lizard, it will stay with you forever. It is just not something you forget (no matter how much you may want to).

So when Sticky uttered "No, *señor!*" the chaos in the pit instantly stopped.

Pablo gasped, "Did you hear that?"

Angelo said, "Oh no!"

Tito cried, "He's here!"

Even the dragon's tongue stopped flicking.

Damien's eyes grew colder and deadlier as he looked around for the source of that unmistakable "No, *señor*!" He, of course, now saw Dave charging forward. So, in true demented-villain fashion, he shouted, "You! Stop or die!"

But, in true teenage fashion, Dave did not stop. He continued running for Sticky, who was struggling toward him, the satchel dragging behind.

"Ah-ha!" Damien cried, and in two big steps, he was upon Sticky.

Damien lifted his boot menacingly.

An evil smirk twisted his already diabolical face as he relished the thought of smashing the sticky-toed nuisance forever.

But (as diabolically demented villains are prone to do) he savored his evil intention a moment too long. And instead of smashing the gecko, *he* came down, tackled by the Bandito Brothers!

Tito grabbed for Sticky but missed.

Damien grabbed for the satchel but instead tore it open, spilling ingots across the sand.

Dave dived in, and as Sticky scampered onto his shoulder, Dave made a desperate grab for the ingots.

He did get one, but only one, and then the dragon charged the skirmishing bodies.

"Help!" the Bandito Brothers cried, scattering in different directions.

Dave rolled away, then stood and saw that the other ingots had been scooped up by Damien Black, who was now talking to the dragon. "Him, my sweet!" he commanded, pointing to Dave. "He is the tasty one. Go!"

The dragon seemed to understand. His tongue flicked in and out quickly. Nervously. He'd had enough of these games. It was time to *eat*.

"You got an ingot, right?" Sticky whispered.

Dave nodded, his eyes on the dragon.

"What are you waiting for? *Ándale!* Put it in!"

Dave slipped his hand inside his sweatshirt.

His hands were shaking, but the ingot snapped in perfectly.

He stood there, waiting for something to happen.

"Are we invisible?" he whispered.

"No, *señor*."

"How do I fly?" he asked, his heart pounding.

"Think like a fly?" Sticky said.

"Think like a fly? How do I do that?"

"I don't know! Buzz in your head?"

Dave tried buzzing in his head. Nothing happened.

The dragon crouched.

Dave broke into a cold sweat.

The powerband didn't work!

They were doomed!

Chapter 11
CROUCHING DRAGON, LYING BOY

The powerband did, indeed, work. Dave just didn't know which power he had.

It wasn't invisibility, that was clear.

It also, quite obviously, wasn't flying.

And faced with a crouching Komodo dragon, Dave could think of only one thing to do.

Run!

I should pause here to explain that running from a Komodo dragon is a futile exercise that will only delay the inevitable. A Komodo dragon can run up to twelve miles an hour, so unless you can run faster than a five-minute mile, it will catch you with its talon-like claws and rip you to shreds with its curved, serrated teeth.

Not a very pleasant way to go, I'm sure you'll agree.

But what else could Dave do?

He ran, and when he did, so did the dragon.

"Ay-ay-ay-ay-ay-ay-ay!" Sticky cried, for the dragon was closing in, and they were trapped!

"Bwaa-ha-ha-ha-ha-ha-ha!" Damien laughed, for the dragon was closing in, and they were trapped!

But then something unexpected happened. Dave suddenly turned and faced the slick, curved wall of the dragon pit and scurried up it with ease.

Dave was too scared and shocked and flabbergasted to say "Huh?" but he was most certainly thinking "Huh?"

As were the Bandito Brothers below.

And also the dragon, who clawed at the wall, furious over losing his dinner.

But Damien Black knew exactly what had

happened—that blasted boy had snagged the Wall-Walker ingot! "Stop him!" Damien cried

at the Bandito Brothers. "A lifetime of gold if you stop him!" (Which really meant that he would kill them shortly after they caught Dave so that he would, in fact, be keeping his word, yet not have to pay a thing.)

"*Asombroso!*" Sticky cried as they escaped the pit.

Dave did not stop, did not pause, did not mull over facing off with Damien Black to retrieve the other ingots.

No, he ran for his life, lickety-split, up the steep and spiraling stairs.

Past the oozy, slimy walls and scurrying rats and fluttering bats and dreadful, dangling spiders.

Through the trapdoor and into the map room.

Out of the map room and down the dingy, dusty, cobwebby maze of creepy corridors.

Past Rosie and the heap of thistly, thorny weeds.

Into the room with floured floors.

Through the door and into the painted elevator (which Dave was now able to just walk down the sides of).

That brought them to the room with nine doors.

Oh yeah, Dave thought, panting. Nine doors and no way out.

"Whatever!" he cried, and bashed the main door with his foot.

It flew open, the shrunken heads clonking and

bonking as Dave and Sticky ran past the cavern of stalagmites and -actites.

Through the crunchy, sloooopy, gross, and goopy waterfall of snails.

Into the foul and fiendish cave (which, at that point, seemed neither particularly foul nor fiendish).

Through the fluttery, stinky bats.

And out into the forest.

And what a relief the forest was!

The fresh air! The towering trees! The hooting owls!

"Quick, *señor*!" Sticky whispered. "Escape while you can! That madman is not far behind, I guarantee!"

So Dave started up again. He ran through the forest, squeezed past the gate, hopped on his bike, and raced down the mountain.

As he rode, he watched his back. He watched the skies. He watched for anything and everything that might be Damien Black following him.

He saw nothing, and at last he was into the heart of the city, dodging traffic. Through the city he zoomed, into his neighborhood, onto his street, and, finally, he was home.

He hopped the curb, yanked open the door to his building, rolled his bike inside, then stood against the row of apartment mailboxes, panting.

"Hopping *habañeros*!" Sticky gasped. "You're a demon on that bike!"

Dave's eye caught on the dusty wall clock ticking lazily above them. "Midnight? How can it be midnight?"

"Well, *señor*, let's see," Sticky said, tapping his chin with his finger. "First we went—"

"Never mind!" Dave snapped, hefting his bike onto one shoulder and charging for the stairwell. "The point is, I'm in trouble! I'm baked! Man, am I dead!"

"Not dead, *señor*. Dead is what you would have been if you hadn't gotten away from that nasty dragon!"

Much the way Dave had had no experience with Komodo dragons, Sticky had no experience with worried mothers. Over the few weeks he'd stayed with Dave's family, he'd seen Dave's mother annoyed (when Dave had neglected to take out the trash) and upset (when Dave had been rude to his sister), but he'd never seen her mad with worry. (And, as you most certainly know from your own experience, there is nothing more frightening than a mother who is mad with worry.)

The attack began when they sneaky-toed through the door.

"Where have you *been?*" his mother cried. "I've been worried sick!" (Which is a mother's way of saying that she's gone mad with worry.)

Dave put down his bike. "I'm *really* sorry, Mom. I got lost."

"Lost? *Lost?* How could you be lost? Where did you go? Why didn't you call?"

Dave was suddenly exhausted. He peeled off his backpack and dumped it on the floor. "I'm sorry," he said feebly.

"Look at your backpack! It's covered in . . . ooooh . . . what *is* that?"

"Da-vy's in trou-ble," a young girl's voice singsonged from the darkness of a bedroom.

"Hush, Evie!" Dave's mother said. Then she saw Dave's back and shoulders. "Are these *cobwebs?*" Her face pinched. "And why do you smell so bad?"

Poor Dave. In his hurry to escape Damien Black and get home safely, he'd forgotten to come up with an explanation. Some believable excuse for being away so long.

In short, he hadn't prepared a lie.

"You've been acting strange for weeks, Dave. You talk to yourself and you've become so secretive.

And now you're out until midnight? What is going on with you? I demand to know!"

Dave weighed the options.

The truth (he'd followed a kleptomaniacal talking gecko lizard into a madman's mansion, where he'd almost been killed by a Komodo dragon) or a lie (like, say, he'd fallen into a gully of slippery, slimy goo, with, oh, cobwebs and . . . uh . . . a scary snake that had wrapped him by the ankle and held him captive for hours).

The lie, it was clear to Dave, was much more believable.

"I fell into a gully of slippery, slimy goo with cobwebs and a snake. A big anaconda kind of snake that wrapped me by the ankle and held me down for hours! I almost died!"

"An anaconda? Where?" Dave's mother asked, concern suddenly filling her eyes.

"Da-vy is ly-ing," his sister singsonged.

"Just ground him," his father growled from

114

across the tiny apartment. Then he snorted, "An anaconda."

"It might have been a boa constrictor! I don't know! All I know is it tried to kill me!"

"Da-vy is ly-ing."

"Shut up, Evie!"

"You shut up, Dave!"

"Both of you, be quiet!" Dave's father shouted. "I've got to go to work in a few hours!" Then he called, "You're grounded, Dave. All weekend. Now go to bed."

Dave was suddenly greatly relieved.

He was grounded!

Damien Black would never find him in this little apartment, in this part of town.

He felt really, truly, amazingly safe!

Ah, how naïve all-knowing thirteen-year-old boys can be.

Chapter 12
ENTER THE CAT

There is no greater punishment than being trapped in a tiny apartment with a hugely annoying sister. Evie was like a pesky fly, buzzing around Dave, singsonging her comments in a way that only annoying little sisters can.

Come to think of it, she was more like a buzzing mosquito.

Her attacks were sharp, sneaky, and persistent.

And she was definitely after blood.

Dave's parents didn't seem to see her attacks. All they saw was Dave swatting her away.

"Just leave her alone, Dave!" his mother said. "Don't go anywhere near her!"

Poor Dave. This was not the sort of strategy

that worked with mosquitoes. Try as he might to avoid her, she found him, attacked, and flew off.

So it didn't take long for Dave to get over his elation at being grounded. It took even less time for him to get over his elation at having survived his encounter with Damien Black. All he could think about was how he'd risked life and limb for the absurd ability to walk on walls.

It was lame.

Stupid.

A joke, not a power.

And it wasn't even enough of a joke to play on his pesky little sister. She wouldn't be scared or wowed or even stunned. She'd just call, "Mo-om, Dave's putting his hands and feet all over the wa-alls! Mo-om!"

Ah, such punishment indeed.

And so it was that Dave brooded the weekend away. He brooded about not being able to fly. About not being able to disappear. About his pesky sister and his disbelieving parents. After all, if they didn't believe him about Evie, how would they ever believe him about Sticky? (For, if you recall, Sticky had made it very clear that if Dave ever told anyone about his ability to talk, Sticky would simply stop talking.)

But as the weekend dragged on, he found himself brooding more and more about Sticky. That lousy lizard wasn't stuck in a tiny apartment with an annoying sister, he was outside sunning himself in the flower box that hung from the kitchen window. He was enjoying himself! Relaxing!

And yes, filling up on bugs.

At last Dave became so annoyed by the klepto-gecko's carefree behavior that he leaned out the window and whispered, "What are you *doing?*"

Sticky eyed him. "What am I doing?" He stretched. "Having a sizzly siesta, *señor!*" He snuggled into the warm dirt and said, "Come on out. Hang on the wall awhile. The sun is *morrocotudo!*"

Dave didn't care how fabulous Sticky thought the sun was. The lizard's whole attitude was burning him up!

"Hang on the wall awhile? I can't hang on the wall awhile! Someone'll see me! Now, maybe if I could fly or go invisible, *that* would be useful. But no, all I can do is walk up a stupid wall!"

Sticky shrugged. "It was your choice, *señor*, not mine."

"It wasn't my choice! It's all I could grab!"

"Still," Sticky said in a nonchalant manner, "you were the one doing the grabbing."

This, of course, was true. But when you're a grounded thirteen-year-old boy trapped in a tiny apartment with disbelieving parents and a mosquito-like sister, you're not what one might call rational.

Truth be told, you're quite *ir*rational.

Unreasonable.

Bad-tempered.

In short, impossible to deal with.

And this irrational, unreasonable, bad-tempered, impossible-to-deal-with thirteen-year-old boy came right out and said what he was thinking: "You know what? I've had nothing but *bad* luck since I saved you from that cat."

Sticky said, "Ah, you cut me to the quick, *señor,*" but he said it in a sunny, funny way. Like nothing was going to ruin his sizzly siesta. Not even insults.

Now, the cat to which Dave referred happened to live right next door. She was fluffy and white, with the eyes of a tiger and a temper to match. Her name was Topaz, and she would have been a pretty cat, except for one thing.

She had a squooshed-in face.

You've seen this sort of face. Some dogs have it, some cats have it, and yes, some people have it. It's the sort of face that looks like it has suffered repeated collisions with windows or doors or, more likely, solid brick walls. It's not the sort of face you would want for yourself, as it's even hard to tolerate on someone else.

But Topaz had such a face, which perhaps explains why she was such an ill-tempered cat. A bad mood would seem to go hand in hand with a squooshed-in face.

It would also seem to go hand in hand with being an outdoor cat trapped indoors.

Topaz, you see, was permanently grounded. The only outside she got near was the breeze through the opening in her owners' kitchen window. A kitchen window that was located (due to kitchen plumbing conveniences) alongside Dave's family's kitchen window.

And it just so happens that while the grounded Dave was whispering to Sticky, the grounded Topaz was sunning herself on the sill of her owners' kitchen window, listening.

Now, don't worry. I am not going to tell you

that the cat could hear and understand and speak. This is, after all, a true story, and everyone knows that cats don't speak.

They can, however, hear sounds, and they do recognize familiar sounds. Sounds such as the neighbor boy talking to the flower box.

Again.

Cats also have very good memories. And what this particular cat on this particular sill remembered was that the last time the boy was talking to the flower box, she had managed to get outside and almost caught one fat and (surely) tasty lizard.

The memory made her pace the windowsill. Made her mew pitifully. And that pitiful mewing is what brought Lily, the sassy, saucy, thirteen-year-old girl who lived there, to the window.

"Whatssamatter, sweetie?" she purred to her kitty (whom she found adorable, despite the tiger-temper and squooshed-in face). And that's when she heard Dave's voice scolding the flower box.

Again.

What a geeky, dorky weirdo, she thought. And since geeky, dorky weirdos are too easy a target for sassy, saucy girls to resist, she lifted the window farther and called out, "Talking to yourself again, Dave?"

Well! There went Topaz, like a bolt of fuzzy, squooshy-faced lightning! Out the window, across the flower box, and then *whoosh*, over seven stories of nothingness (into which you and I would have plummeted to our deaths) and onto Dave's flower box.

"Catch her!" the sassy, saucy girl cried. "Grab her quick before she falls!"

The minute Sticky saw Topaz coming, he abandoned his siesta and zoomed lickety-split across the box and up Dave's arm. "*Ay caramba!*" he panted. "Here we go again!"

"Grab her, Dave! Grab her!"

Sticky's preference would have been to let the

cat fall on its face, but it would have made no difference (to its face, anyway).

Besides, cats have nine lives.

She would be back.

"Dave, what are you waiting for? Grab her!"

Evie was at the window now, singing, "Davy's got a girlfriend, Davy's got a girlfriend!"

"Shut up, Evie!" Dave snapped, lunging for the cat. He snagged her by the nape of the neck and hauled her in, clawing and mewing like she was being tortured. (Which, in fact, she was not. She was just furious that she'd missed the lizard again.)

Dave held her out like a furry, clawy, stinky diaper and met Lily in the hallway. "Oh, thank you! Thank you so much!" she gushed, acting neither sassy nor saucy.

"*Hasta la vista*, uuuuuugly," Sticky muttered at the cat from inside Dave's sweatshirt.

"What did you say?" Lily asked.

"Huh? Oh." Dave cleared his throat. "Hasta

be awfully hard for her, being cooped up inside all day."

Lily smoothed back Topaz's fur, making the cat's flat face seem even squooshier. "Don't I know," she grumbled. "I'm grounded for grades." She gave him a sassy, saucy smirk. "Why are you home? Don't you have rounds to make, delivery boy?"

She was making fun of his after-school job, but this was nothing new. And he might have said, I don't do deliveries on weekends, but instead, something inside him made him want to brag.

"Nah. I'm grounded, too."

Her eyebrows shot up. "You? *Grounded?*"

He nodded, pleased with her reaction. "Got home too late on Friday night." He turned to go back into his apartment. "Well, see you at school tomorrow," he said, then left her in the hallway with her jaw dangling.

It was enough to make him forget all about his

troubles. You see, in addition to being a sassy, saucy thirteen-year-old, Lily Espinoza was quite a looker. One of those girls whose mere presence turns ordinarily coordinated boys into blushing, bumbling fools.

But for once Dave hadn't stuttered in her presence.

He hadn't tripped.

Hadn't bashed into her with his bike.

For once he'd been smooth. (Or, as Sticky might say, *suavecito!*)

Yes, at that moment, the Bandito Brothers and Damien Black were the furthest things from his mind.

Too bad for Dave, he was the only thing on theirs.

Chapter 13
MEANWHILE, BACK AT THE MANSION

Meanwhile, back at the mansion, Damien Black had survived his own dragon's attack. So, too, had the Bandito Brothers, but that was only because they had traded their lives for loyalty. (Which is to say they were now firmly aligned with the evil treasure hunter.) (And *that* is to say they'd promised to help Damien find the boy.)

But where to begin?

Damien Black's mansion loomed behind the city in an otherwise uninhabited area known as Raven Ridge. Like an eerie shadow, it was present yet overlooked by people as they hustled and bustled through their lives. A tingling of the spine, a sudden chill or a shiver . . . these were felt by the people of the city, but they were largely shaken off, dismissed, or ignored.

It was only if one paused to consider the shiver, paused to look up at the house, that the source was revealed. The house was, as you already know, wholly and totally spooky. But it's a well-known fact that adults don't buy into wholly and totally spooky. They buy into terms like "antique" or "fixer-upper" or "old and decrepit." (Perhaps because they, too, are becoming old and decrepit, and would rather be viewed as antiques.)

But a young person calls a dog a dog (not a canine or man's best friend or hunny-bunny-poochy-woochy). So a young person calls a wholly and totally spooky house (or person) exactly what it is—wholly and totally spooky.

So the house (and all the activities within) had a certain immunity. Adults ignored it, and children avoided it. This, then, explains how oddly jutting rooms could be built or dungeons created or Komodo dragons introduced, all without notice. It also explains how a telescope of mega-multiplying magnification could poke out of the window of one of those oddly jutting rooms without objection from the neighbors below.

Nobody noticed.

Now, the amount of time it took Dave and Sticky to get out of the mansion and onto the bike was exactly the amount of time it took Damien Black and his new cohorts to get out of the dragon pit and up to the mega-multiplying-magnification telescope (or, as the brass plate on the side of the telescope boasted, the Mighty Triple-M).

Damien put one of his dark and dangerous eyes up to the Mighty Triple-M (which, I think you'll agree, actually makes it a *Quadruple*-M).

He swiftly moved the telescope across the landscape.

"Bwaa-ha-ha!" Damien laughed when he caught

sight of Dave racing off on his bike. "Bwaa-ha-ha-ha-ha-ha-ha!"

"You spotted him, Mr. Black?"

The treasure hunter raised an eyebrow in Pablo's direction as if to say, Why *else* would I be bwaa-ha-ha'ing, you fool? then resumed tracking the boy with his Mighty Triple-M.

"What does he have, anyway?" Angelo asked.

"What are those coins about?" Pablo added.

"They were very shiny!" Tito said with a head-bobby nod.

Again, Damien gave them a look. A long, hard, dark look, which meant, Ask any more questions and I'll feed you to the dragon.

The Brothers took a step back.

Even Tito gulped.

Damien continued to stare until, with a jolt, he realized that his long, hard, dark look had gone on way too long. What if the boy had gotten

MIGHTY TRIPLE "M"

away? He quickly turned back to his scope, and when he found Dave again, he began muttering things like "You pesky little thief! You rotten little robber! You bungling burglar! You burrito bandito!"

"Hey!" the Bandito Brothers cried, for they

were sensitive to such insensitive remarks, even if they weren't directed directly at them.

But the treasure hunter ignored their complaint and went on, his voice getting louder and more high-pitched as he trained the scope on Dave. "You crooked crook!" (As if there is such a thing as a straight crook?) "You pint-sized pickpocket! You nettling nuisance! You tricky trespasser! You confounded *brat*!"

And that's what was really at the heart of the matter. You see, Damien Black had never been outsmarted by anyone.

Anyone besides Sticky, that is.

But still. It was one thing to be outsmarted by a talking lizard. The gecko, he assumed, was most likely bewitched or in possession of supernatural powers.

But being outsmarted by a boy?

A crummy, scrawny *boy*?

It was an insult!

A slap in the dastardly face!

(And if there's one thing a maniacal demon of a man cannot take, it's a slap in his dastardly face.)

So Damien Black watched Dave through the powerful lens, following him off the mountain, across the river, and into the city, vowing to catch him.

Cage him!

Take the powerband from him and have his revenge!

He did manage to track him for quite a distance inside the city, but even the mightiest of mega-multiplying-magnification telescopes can't see around corners, so at last he lost sight of him.

"To the map room!" he cried, and off they all scurried, through secret passages, down a rope ladder, along a pulley cart, inside a vacuum tube, up through the trapdoor, and into the map room.

With great flair, Damien pulled down a detailed map of the area and stood staring at it as he twisted his mustache and murmured such things as "Hmm-mm. Ahhhh. Hmmm."

Finally Pablo dared to speak. "What are you thinking, Mr. Black?"

This made Angelo brave a question, too. "Do you have an idea where he might be?"

Damien did not raise an eyebrow in their direction.

He did not sneer or snap or shout.

He simply nodded.

Then he picked up a pointer and thwapped it against the map. "I lost sight of him here." He dragged the pointer, zigzagging along roads until he reached a neighborhood on the outskirts of town. "This area *here* is a possibility," he said, circling it with his pointer. "Or *here*," he said, circling another neighborhood.

"How do you know, Mr. Black? How can you tell?"

Again, there was no shouting, no snapping, no

raising of eyebrows. There was simply a smirk and a twist of the mustache as he replied, "Because no boy with money would risk his life that way."

The smirk grew.

The twisting of the mustache became extra twisty.

And in his fiendish eyes, the Bandito Brothers could see a devilish glint forming.

Damien Black had a plan.

A dastardly, dark, diabolical plan.

Chapter 14
DELIVERY BOY

Dave did not think of himself as poor. (Of course, those who are rich with a family's love never do.) His father worked at the neighborhood market, his mother at a Laundromat. "Your dad and I are a good team," Dave's mother would say. "Between the two of us, you're always clean and fed."

So Dave didn't notice that the streets in his neighborhood were narrow and crowded or that nobody drove fancy cars. He also didn't think twice that the playing fields at school were more dirt than grass. Or that his principal made the morning announcements through a megaphone from the middle rung of an A-frame ladder.

Ms. Batista was, after all, a little bit quirky.

It wasn't until he began couriering—or delivery-boying, as Lily would say—that he started noticing how different life was outside his neighborhood.

Now, you may be wondering how a boy like Dave, whose father works at a corner market and whose mother works at a Laundromat, gets a job *couriering* envelopes between businesses and banks and restaurants in the hustling, bustling heart of the city.

It would, after all, be a reasonable thing to wonder.

And I could give you a lengthy, detailed explanation, but instead, I'll simply say this: the school librarian, Mr. Kelly, got him the job.

Hmm. Perhaps you do need to know just a *little* bit more.

Mr. Kelly's official title was library media specialist, for although the school did not have an adequate public address system, it did, in fact, have a few computers in its library. And it was on one of these computers (the main one) that Mr. Kelly discovered a message that had been forwarded via the school district's communication lines. It was a message originated by City Bank looking for a bike-riding student who would work as a courier.

"They want someone quick, punctual, tidy, and reliable," Mr. Kelly had told Dave. "Sounds like you to me."

Dave hadn't known what to think, as he was, at this time, still twelve (and not yet an all-knowing thirteen-year-old). Up to now his job had been to get good grades. His dad had always told him, "School is your job and your only job, son. Prove yourself at this one and you'll be a rich executive someday!"

But Mr. Kelly had taken out a map and said, "Here's City Bank. All they want is for you to make deliveries to places around town. I've seen you ride that bike of yours—you could handle this easily." Then he leaned in and said, "Dave, they'll pay ten dollars per delivery!"

That afternoon, Dave reported to City Bank.

And yes, the woman at the bank was surprised to see a boy so young, but there he was, punctual, tidy, and (so far) reliable. So she gave him a shot. And when Dave's father saw the extra twenty dollars on the dinner table that night and heard how it had gotten there, he sat for a very long time just chewing and thinking.

At last he said, "If you are going to do this, I think you should start a business and do it right. Business cards, a shirt, everything." He gave Dave a stern look. "But if your grades start to slip, that's it."

This, then, is how Dave formed Roadrunner Express. He kept his grades up, his hair trimmed, and his clothes neat. His orders came in through Mr. Kelly's computer, and every day when the dismissal bell rang, he pulled on a red ROADRUNNER EXPRESS sweatshirt (which his mother had embroidered), clipped on his helmet, and pedaled into the city to courier envelopes for a growing number of customers.

It's why the kids at school always called "Meep-meep!" when he raced by.

It's also why girls like Lily thought he was a buttoned-up dork.

Now, by the time Sticky came into his life, Dave had been delivering envelopes and packages for at least six months. His deliveries had taken him through every street in the city and out to nearly every neighborhood. He had met a lot of people, and it had opened his eyes to things such as luxury cars and golf courses and private helicopters and sushi bars. (Not to mention hoboes and hustlers and piles of stinky garbage and people who seemed certifiably crazy.)

But in all his days delivering, there was one thing Dave had never seen. One thing that, when he did see it, struck terror in his heart in a way that not even hoboes and hustlers and certifiably crazy people can.

A mariachi band.

Dave skidded to a halt about a block away. "Sticky!" he whispered into his sweatshirt.

"*Sí, señor?*" Sticky answered with a yawn and a lazy stretch, for while Dave had been racing around town, he'd been enjoying a siesta.

Then he heard the music. "Ay-ay-ay!" he said, poking his head out. "There's only one band that plays that bad!"

It was true.

The band was screechy.

Out of tune.

Out of time!

And their singing was terrible!

"What are they doing here?" Dave whispered.

"What do you think, *señor*?" And then, because Dave was just staring, Sticky shrugged and said, "They are looking for you." His little gecko head bobbed like he'd been expecting this all along. "And for me."

They watched the Bandito Brothers speak with people on the street, then move on, strumming their guitars.

Dave turned into a side street, keeping in the shadows as he watched the Brothers. "But the city is huge! How do they ever expect to find us?"

Sticky pursed his little gecko lips.

He pulled them back tight.

He moved them to the right, to the left, and back again.

And at last he frowned and said, "Most *hombres* would have shown off their gecko powers by now."

"Gecko powers? *Gecko* powers? Is that what you call it?" Dave snorted. "What's to show off?"

But it was true. Most boys would have climbed

every wall in the neighborhood. Hung from every ceiling they could find. Scared their teachers. Impressed their friends. Done *something* with the ability. But all Dave could think about was what he couldn't do.

He couldn't fly.

He couldn't go invisible.

He couldn't even lift heavy things.

All he could do was walk on walls.

Big deal.

And sure, he had used it a couple of times. Once at school to get a ball off the cafeteria roof and once at home to freak his sister out. But at school he'd been careful that no one saw, and at home it had not had the desired effect.

"Show-off" is all Evie had said before huffing off.

And now Dave was glad that he hadn't shown off more. He'd naïvely thought that his battle with Damien Black was over, but now he could see that he'd underestimated the determination of the dastardly, demented villain. (And if there's one thing you should never do, it's underestimate the determination of dastardly, demented villains.)

Sticky saw the gears in Dave's mind connecting. Saw the reality of the situation dawning on him. "You look a little green, *señor*."

Dave *was* a little green. "He's never going to stop looking for it, is he?" he whispered.

"Never," Sticky said.

"What am I going to *do*?"

It was a good question.

A very good question indeed.

Sticky pursed his lips.

He tapped his chin.

And as the Bandito Brothers moved their loud, screechy, out-of-time, out-of-tune show farther along the street, he said, "I think, *señor*, it's time for you to get a disguise."

Chapter 15
THE DISGUISE

Perhaps you're wondering why Dave didn't just chuck the powerband into the river and be done with it.

He did, in fact, consider it. But then he realized that Damien Black would not know he had done this. Damien Black would still be after him!

Or perhaps you're wondering why Dave didn't turn the powerband over to the police and tell them everything.

He considered that, too. But in the end, he just couldn't seem to part with it. After all, he finally admitted, even a lame power such as the ability to walk on walls was better than no power at all.

And what if someday, some way, he could get his hands on the other ingots?

What if someday, some way, he really could *fly*?

So instead of chucking the powerband into the river or turning it over to the police, he did what any boy in his predicament would do.

He bought sunglasses.

Sunglasses and hats and T-shirts.

Now, granted, these things do not make for much of a disguise. But as I have said before, this is not a made-up story. This is a real story about a real boy, and real boys do not dress in shiny, stretchy fabrics sewn into embarrassingly tight and wholly ridiculous costumes. Real boys avoid shiny, stretchy fabrics at all costs. Real boys like sunglasses, hats, and T-shirts.

Sticky watched patiently as Dave tried on every combination of hat, shirt, and sunglasses. But at last he said, "If you ask me, *hombre*, it's the shoes that give you away. *Those* are what that evil *hombre* will recognize. And that backpack. And you should never wear that snake hat again."

Dave blinked at his feet, then at the gecko. The shoes were his only pair, but Sticky was right. The red trim made them distinctive. He had to get rid of them. And the backpack. And especially the hat!

So the next day Dave bought more shoes.

A different backpack.

And (because they were right there at the checkout stand) bandannas.

Then he ditched his old shoes, the hat, and his old backpack in a garbage can, went home, locked himself in the bathroom, and tried new ways of disguising himself.

He cut holes and made a mask out of one of the bandannas.

"This looks so lame!" he moaned.

Sticky nodded. "*Mucho* lame-o."

He tied a bandanna across his nose and mouth.

"Now I look like a bank robber!"

"*Sí, señor,* you do."

Now, to his credit, Dave had never considered using his wall-walking power for evil. Or even just bad. It had never even crossed his mind that he could scale buildings, sneak in through windows, steal things, and leave. Dave may have been an all-knowing thirteen-year-old boy, but he was a hardworking, *good* thirteen-year-old boy. Going into other people's houses to steal things was just not something he would do.

(Hmm. Yes, he *had* been persuaded to sneak into a monstrous mansion by a kleptomaniacal talking gecko lizard, but that was an exception.)

Sticky, on the other hand, enjoyed scaling walls at night, finding sparkly things in other people's apartments, and adding them to his secret treasure stash behind the bookshelf in Dave's room. The thrill of bringing something new home (regardless of its actual value) gave him great satisfaction.

But the more he was around Dave, the less Sticky ventured out at night. Sticky was almost puzzled by how Dave was nothing like the Bandito Brothers or Damien Black. He wasn't deceptive or double-crossing. He wasn't nice one minute and mean the next. He wasn't crazed for power or consumed by greed. He was just a boy. A good, hard-working boy.

So it was with a deep breath and a puffy-cheeked sigh that Sticky finally said to Dave (who was still playing around with his robber bandanna), "Look, *señor*, the idea is to cover up, not stick out like you're going to stick 'em up." Then he added (almost hopefully), "Unless you're thinking you might do a stick-'em-up?"

Dave whipped off the bandanna. "No!"

Now, right on the other side of the bathroom door was an ear. A big ear attached to the head of a little girl with a big mouth. And suddenly the fist attached to this little girl's arm pounded on the door, and the big mouth cried, "Who is that? Who are you talking to?"

"Me, myself, and I," Dave shot back. "Now leave me alone!"

"I need to use the bathroom."

"No, you don't! Leave me alone!"

But Evie, pesky little sister that she was, did not know how to leave her brother alone. What she did know, however, was how to tattle.

"Mo-om! Dave's talking to himself again! Mo-om! Dave won't get out of the bathroom! Mo-om!"

So Dave muttered, "Forget it!" and shoved everything inside his backpack.

Still, something about having a disguise (lame as it might have been) made Dave feel safer. He had no idea when he would ever need it, but there it was, in his new backpack, ready to conceal him at a moment's notice.

Meanwhile, across town, a truly poor boy named Luis happened upon a pair of tennis shoes while digging through garbage cans. He turned them over, not believing his luck. The shoes were worn but wonderful, with red piping and fat red laces.

He turned back to the trash bin.

There was a backpack, too!

A perfectly good (although well-worn and somewhat soiled) backpack!

And a super-cool ball cap with a radical diamondback snake design.

In his entire life, Luis had never felt this lucky.

He put on the shoes and the cap and strutted down the street feeling happy and extremely hip.

Poor, unlucky Luis.

He now looked just like Dave.

Chapter 16
MARIACHI SPIES

Luis, of course, did not look *just* like Dave. He may have had the same dark hair, but he was smaller and younger, with a broader nose, more closely set eyes, and rather large, floppy earlobes.

But to the Bandito Brothers (who saw no value in children) and Damien Black (to whom children were like cat-sized rats—vermin that were both interchangeable and expendable), Luis could easily be mistaken for Dave.

And that is exactly what happened one afternoon as the Bandito Brothers were strumming and strolling near Luis's neighborhood (working their way, day by day, ever closer to Dave's).

"Look!" Pablo gasped, reining back Rosie. "It's him!"

Angelo stopped mid-strum. "Finally!"

Tito, though, being quite childlike himself, studied the boy walking along the street and said, "That's not him. His earlobes are too big."

"Earlobes?" Pablo asked with a squint. *"Earlobes?"*

"You idiot!" Angelo said, thumping the back of Tito's head with his guitar.

"Ow!" Tito complained, but Pablo was already pulling a walkie-talkie out of his holster.

Now, when I say "walkie-talkie," I don't mean the sort of slick model an ordinary person might purchase at an ordinary store. No, this particular walkie-talkie was a strange-looking contraption made by Damien Black himself. It was fashioned out of odds and ends, bits and pieces, and, of course, gizmos and gadgets and thingamajiggies.

It had the handle of a flashlight (so it fit quite

nicely into the six-shooter holster), but other than that, it wasn't like anything you've ever seen before. It had wires and glowing tubes and antennas, a rubbery ear on the side, and a mouthpiece in front with *lips*.

Pablo switched on the power.

He extended a long, spirally antenna.

Folded out a grid-shaped doohickey.

Spread out a fan-shaped thingamabob.

Dialed a frequency knob until it was lined up with a picture of the mansion.

And at last he whispered into the rubbery ear.

"Mr. Black," he hissed. "Come in, Mr. Black!"

He waited a moment for a reply, and when there

wasn't one, he tried again. "Mr. Black! Come in, Mr. Black! We have found the boy!"

Suddenly there was a snap.

A crackle.

A pop!

And then the raspy voice of Damien Black came (quite eerily) through the lips. "Are you certain?"

Tito rolled his eyes and shook his head, but Pablo hissed, "Yes!" into the ear. "Come quickly! He's walking toward downtown."

"Follow him!" Damien's voice commanded. "I've got your coordinates. I'll be right there!" Then the lips shouted, "And leave the communicator on, you fools!"

Now, when Damien Black says he'll be right there, trust me, he'll be right there. Not in a car or a plane or a helicopter, and certainly not on a buck-toothed burro. No, the way Damien Black moves from his monstrous mansion on the top of Raven

Ridge to anywhere in the city in a lickety-split get-there-quick sort of fashion is on his motorcycle.

Now, again. This is a Damien Black contraption, not one made by, say, Harley-Davidson. It's small, like a moped, but with gadgets galore and ape-hanger handlebars (because even dangerous, demented villains have their sense of style). It's black (for stealth in the night) and has a wicked rocket fuel–injected motor that can propel it from zero to one fifty in four point six seconds while sending bright orange flames out its twin exhaust pipes.

It is, in a word, bad.

And although most motorists would take the road to get to or from Raven Ridge, Damien Black was not most motorists. He was a diabolically demented villain, and diabolically demented villains prefer shortcuts when hurrying to perform diabolically demented deeds.

Damien Black had such a shortcut.

He hadn't built it himself. He had just connected to it via a ramp beneath the dungeon.

It was a shortcut that went under the city.

A shortcut that was wet.

And stinky.

A shortcut that most people would never consider taking themselves.

A shortcut known to the rest of the city as . . . the sewer system.

Now, because Damien Black lived among bats and rats and Komodo dragons, he did not mind the stench. He also did not mind the wetness, as he could tear right through it on his motorcycle when it was shallow, and if it got too deep, the wheels of his motorcycle turned sideways, transforming the machine into a sewage-spewing Jet Ski (which had the tendency to put the kibosh on anyone chasing him).

So it was with great speed that Damien Black left his mansion and traveled under the city toward the Bandito Brothers.

It was, however, *not* with great speed or stealth that the Bandito Brothers followed Luis down the street. They were, after all, on foot, dragging along guitars and a bucktoothed burro.

But even without the guitars or the burro, they were just not that sneaky.

In fact, they were bumbly.

Stumbly.

And they said "Shh!" to each other so many times that Luis finally noticed that he was being followed.

Now, if you were being followed by bumbly, stumbly banditos with a bucktoothed burro, you would, at first, think the same thing Luis thought:

What a joke.

But if those bumbly, stumbly banditos and that bucktoothed burro tailed you up one street and down another, across a park, and over a bridge, you might start to get nervous and wonder, as Luis did, what the heck was going on.

"Hey, you weirdos!" he finally called out to them. "Why are you following me?"

"We are just going the same way as you!" Angelo called back.

"And we are not weirdos!" Pablo shouted.

Tito nodded. "We're a mariachi band!"

This made Luis snort and roll his eyes, and for a moment he felt better.

But then he turned around and saw a manhole cover in front of him wobble and scrape to the side.

A dark-haired man with a twisty mustache and dangerous eyes emerged from underground.

The man sneered at him as he leapt to the street.

And in that instant, Luis understood.

He was in deep, diabolical doo-doo.

Chapter 17
OVER THE EDGE

Being in deep, diabolical doo-doo causes the same reaction in all young boys.

They run!

But (after a short delay caused by his ape-hanger handlebars getting tangled in the manhole opening) Damien zoomed after him.

The Bandito Brothers piled onto Rosie any way they could, then joined the hot pursuit with Angelo shouting "Giddyap!" as Pablo mercilessly slapped the poor burro's behind with his guitar.

And Luis might have escaped, but he made the mistake of *thinking* he'd escaped. (And if there's another thing you should never do, it's think you've escaped while you're still escaping.)

Around one corner he flew, breathlessly checking behind him for the devilish moped man or the weridos on the bucktoothed burro.

They were nowhere in sight.

Around the next corner he flew, and again, no devil on a moped or bucktoothed burro.

Around the *third* corner he flew, and it was here that Luis, gasping for breath, finally believed he was safe.

Poor, poor Luis. He didn't realize he had circled the block!

And when he stopped looking over his shoulder and instead looked ahead, he bumped right into the devilish moped man.

"Aaaaaaah!" Luis screamed.

"Bwaa-ha-ha!" Damien Black laughed, grabbing the boy by the nape of the neck. "Gotcha!"

"Let go, let go!" Luis screamed, kicking and flailing his arms and legs.

It was then that Damien realized that nabbing a

boy by the nape of the neck on a busy street in broad daylight was maybe not such a swift move to make.

So he dragged him, kicking and screaming, across the street to a narrow alleyway between tall buildings. An alleyway with trash cans and mangy cats and broken bottles and not much else.

Unfortunately for Luis, people in the vicinity were distracted by a bucktoothed burro attempting to gallop up the street with three grown mariachi men on its back. And so they were unaware that a young boy was being abducted.

Luis was indeed in danger.

Terrible, mortal danger.

Struggle as he might, he could not free himself from the devilish man's clutches. "Help!" he shouted at the top of his lungs, but Damien just clamped a cruel hand over his mouth and whispered, "Help yourself, you fool. Where is it?"

"Wrar wrar wrar!" Luis cried from behind Damien's hand.

Damien released his grip on Luis's mouth.

"Help!" Luis screamed. "Somebody h—"

Fwap went Damien's hand over his mouth, and this time he shook poor Luis's face as he demanded, "Where is it?"

"Wrar wrar wrar!" Luis cried from behind Damien's hand.

"I'm through playing games!" Damien fumed. He tried to frisk the boy's arms, but with all the flailing Luis was doing, it was impossible to tell anything. So he hauled Luis to a set of fire escape stairs that zigzagged up, up, up for eight floors.

He dragged him to the second level, where he felt it would be safe to slam Luis against the wall and frisk him.

"Hey, you!" someone cried from a window in a building across the alley. "Let him go or I'll call the police!"

It was just the distraction Luis needed to break free. And since Damien was blocking the steps that went down, Luis ran in the only direction he could.

Up.

With each flight, the furious treasure hunter tried to nab him.

With each flight, the boy had only one place to go.

Up.

So up, up, up, up, *up* they both ran, until at last they were on the roof.

"Where are you fools?" Damien screamed into the ear of his communicator. "I need your help!"

But the Bandito Brothers were in no position or condition to help. At that moment, they and their bucktoothed burro were causing a metal-munching, windshield-crunching pileup in the street.

SCREECH!

BAM!

CRUNCH!

WHAM!

One car after another collided, until the whole intersection was blocked.

"Uh-oh," Pablo said.

"Not good," Angelo agreed.

"Should we maybe play a happy song?" Tito asked, looking around at the wreckage that surrounded them.

Pablo and Angelo exchanged looks, then jumped off of Rosie and scrambled through the jumble of bumpers and broken glass, leaving Tito and Rosie to fend for themselves.

Meanwhile, Damien had chased Luis around the roof of the building until at last he had him cornered. "Now!" he panted. "Give it to me or *die*."

"I don't know what you're talking about!" Luis cried.

Damien grabbed him by the neck and gave him a diabolical sneer. "What do you take me for? A fool?"

"NO!" Luis choked out. "I take you for a crazy man!"

Damien pinched the boy's neck tighter and ripped off his shirtsleeve.

No powerband.

He ripped off the other sleeve.

Again, no powerband.

"Where is it?" he shouted.

Then a giant lightbulb went on over his devious, diabolical head.

"Bwaa-ha-ha-ha-ha!" he cried, then grabbed the boy by the ankle, dragged him onto the ground, turned him onto his stomach, and sat on him while he inspected his ankles.

His pockets!

His armpits!

"Where is it?" he finally screeched. "Where have you hidden it?"

"I don't know!" Luis said into the gravelly roof.

"Well, let's see if we can't make you remember!" Damien snarled.

And with that, he grabbed the boy by his ankles, hung him upside down, waddled him across the roof, and did something only a desperate, diabolical demon of a man would do.

He dangled him over the edge.

Chapter 18
EXTREME GRAVITY

Since the day that Dave had first seen the Bandito Brothers in town, he'd watched for them while he was out making his Roadrunner Express deliveries.

Each time he found them, they had moved closer to his neighborhood.

Each day he saw them, he grew more and more nervous.

And each time Sticky had to tell him, "You would be safer to ignore them, *señor*. They are looking for a boy in red and white sneakers and a snake hat."

But Dave seemed unable to ignore them. He couldn't help wondering if they were asking about a boy with a pet gecko. Sticky had been lying low, but a lot of the kids at school knew he had a pet gecko. A lot of his *neighborhood* knew it.

What if the Bandito Brothers found out where he lived?

What if Damien Black came to his apartment?

What if that demented villain hurt his family?

Well, his sister, that would be one thing. But his parents?

Then one day Dave was racing through the streets on his bike, making a delivery to a business on the outskirts of the city, when he heard the metal-munching, windshield-crunching pileup of cars.

"*Ay caramba!* What was that?" Sticky cried, jolting awake from his siesta.

Dave coasted for a moment, then turned down a side street toward the sound. He could hear people shouting, and everyone on the sidewalks seemed to be funneling toward the commotion.

"What a mess!" Dave said as the intersection came into view.

It wasn't just a two- or three-car crash.

There were cars crunched in all directions.

People were shouting.

Crying.

It was a doozy of a disaster.

And then Sticky choked out, "Hopping *habañeros*! Look!" as he pointed to the very heart of the chaos. "It's Rosie and Tito!"

Now, it's a well-known fact that gravity pulls. There's the gravity of the earth, which keeps us and our buildings and our bikes and burros all securely on the ground. It's a very strong force, and the truth is, no one completely understands it.

A *situation* also has a pull to it, depending on its gravity. It's not the same kind of gravity as the gravity of earth, but it has a similar effect.

People are pulled to it.

The more grave the situation, the stronger the pull. So in this particular case, in this particular city, this particular metal-munching, windshield-crunching pileup had what might be called *extreme* gravity.

Everybody wanted to get a closer look.

Now, when Dave saw that the nucleus of this pileup, the very heart of this pull, was one badly bucktoothed burro, he, too, wanted to get a closer look. But he was encumbered by his bike. So he backtracked to a basement stairwell, locked his bike against the railing, then returned to the chaos in the intersection.

Word of the wreck had radiated out quickly, and more and more people were funneling in to see.

Sirens wailed in the distance.

People began shoving and bumping.

And then a familiar voice called through the crowd, "Dave!"

"Ay *chihuahua*, not her!" Sticky said, ducking for cover.

It was, indeed, Lily, who had spotted Dave's bright red sweatshirt and was now squeezing between people to get to him. "Did you see what happened?"

Dave shook his head.

"What's a *donkey* doing here? And who's that guy on it? Why is he wearing a bandolier? Is that ammunition real? Does he have a gun?"

Dave knew the answers to all these questions (or, at least, he believed he did), but he wisely chose not to answer them. Instead, he did what he usually did when he was around Lily.

He stood there staring at her, feeling totally dorky.

And it was while he was standing there, feeling (and, I'm afraid, *looking*) totally dorky, that something strange happened.

Something very strange indeed.

A hat came out of the sky and landed with a loud *thwap* between Dave and Lily.

It was a purple ball cap.

With a diamondback snake design.

Dave stared, not believing his eyes.

Was this *his* hat?

Lily snatched it off the ground. "Is this *your* hat?" she asked, understandably confused, as Dave was wearing his bike helmet.

"N-no," Dave lied, staring at the hat.

Then Lily looked up. Up to where the hat had thwapped down from. And then Lily, being a very vocal sort of girl, let out an ear-piercing, heart-spearing *scream* as she backed away from the building.

Soon everyone was looking up at the dreadful sight above, talking, pointing, and yes, screaming.

And that's when Sticky, who had been slyly watching the exchange between Dave and Lily,

179

looked up, up, up and saw poor Luis dangling down, down, down from the roof of the building.

"What the *jalapeño* is that?" he cried. But then, because geckos have keen eyesight, he figured out what the *jalapeño* it was. "*Señor! Ay caramba! Señor!*" he said, pulling frantically on Dave's ear. "It's Damien Black!" And then, being one smart gecko, he put it all together lickety-split. "The hat! Hopping *habañeros, hombre*! That evil *hombre*'s got a boy he thinks is you!"

Dave looked around frantically.

There wasn't a policeman in sight!

He could hear sirens, so he knew they were coming (or at least trying to), but by the time they got there, it might be too late.

Someone had to do something!

Why was everyone just standing around?

Then, in his ear, he heard Sticky's voice. "Why are you standing there like a *bobo* saguaro?"

"Huh?"

"You need to move! *Ándale!*"

Dave looked at the gecko. "Move? Move where?"

Sticky blinked at Dave.

He stretched out his little gecko spine.

He crossed his little gecko arms.

Then he gave Dave a stern, hard look and said, "Climb the building, man! Save the boy!"

Chapter 19
A TAKE-TEN-PACES-AND-SHOOT SITUATION

Dave wasted no time. He returned to the basement stairwell where he had chained his bike, hurried down the stairs, and swiftly stripped out of his helmet, sweatshirt, shirt, and shoes. Then he donned a black shirt, a black cap, slip-on shoes, and shades, and stuffed the rest of his belongings inside his backpack, which he left in the corner of the basement stairwell.

If you've ever seen a gecko move, you know they are quick, assured, and nimble. And although Dave moved quickly and nimbly up the wall, he was not feeling at all assured.

"I can't believe I'm up this high!" he said when they'd reached the third floor. "What if the power just *stops*?"

"It won't!" Sticky replied, then mumbled, "At least, it never has for me."

"But you're a gecko! You're *supposed* to walk on walls!"

While he talked, Dave pressed on, moving nimbly on a diagonal across the building toward the side where Damien was dangling Luis from the roof. With each step, he moved more and more in the style of a gecko, holding his arms and legs to the side instead of beneath him. With each step he took, he felt stronger, more agile, more comfortable being on a wall.

Up the building he darted.

Around the corner he scurried.

He could see Damien Black now, could hear him yelling something at the boy.

And below him? Below him people had stopped screaming and were now gasping and asking each other, "How is he climbing the wall? Can you see a rope? Is he a rock climber? Who is that? *What* is that?"

And then came the inevitable moment when Damien saw him.

He stopped shaking Luis.

He blinked his dark, disbelieving eyes at Dave, then uttered the only word appropriate in such a situation:

"Huh?"

But in a flash, his eyes were back to being deadly and diabolical, and he roared, "BWAA-HA-HA-HA-HA-HA-HA!" which echoed eerily off the building across the street. "BWAA-HA-HA-HA-HA-HA-HA!"

You see, in the end, he had found the boy.

The right boy.

His actions had ultimately drawn him out.

(By mistake, perhaps, but to Damien's mind, the result immediately became part of his master plan. His premeditated, brilliant scheme to flush out the boy and get what was rightfully his! Bwaa-ha-ha-ha-ha-ha-ha! This, you see, is how dastardly villains make themselves feel smart.)

And now what?

Dave had no problem with now what. He was filled with a newfound bravery. A power inside of him that made him believe that he could outrun that evil *hombre*, no problem. A power inside of him that made him believe that he was stronger, quicker, faster, and smarter than evil.

He had the power of *good*.

Luis, at this point, however, thought he had lost his mind. It was, after all, flooded with blood from hanging upside down, and that, combined with the fear of dying, made not believing what he was seeing quite believable.

But the vision of a boy walking straight up the wall didn't go away. And then the crazy man who had been dangling him upside down suddenly hoisted him back up onto the roof and dumped him.

As the blood rushed out of his head, he

realized that he *had* seen what he'd thought he'd seen.

A boy had walked up the wall to save him.

The minute Luis had his wits about him and saw that the devilish man was no longer interested in him, he got to his feet and started sneaky-toeing toward the fire escape stairs. But just as he was getting near it, two of the weirdos who had followed him earlier came panting onto the roof.

"Mr. Black!" they shouted. "We're here!"

Damien Black waved them back, as he was crouched and ready to pounce the instant Dave came over the edge.

But once again, Damien Black was about to be outwitted by a child.

(With the help, that is, of a gecko lizard.)

"Careful, *hombre*, careful," Sticky whispered in Dave's ear. "A little to the left, *then* leap up."

So that's what Dave did. And the instant he was on the roof and saw Pablo and Angelo blocking the emergency stairs, he realized that there was only one way down.

The same way he'd come up.

Which he could have turned around and done right then, but there was one little problem.

The boy.

Now, dastardly, demented villains like Damien Black understand that people who are good cannot just abandon people who need help.

Dastardly, demented villains like Damien Black *count* on this.

It's how they lure victims into their lairs.

How they extract information.

How they use people to get the things they want.

And what Damien Black wanted more than anything he'd ever wanted was to get the powerband back.

So he moved toward Dave and said, "There's no way out. Give it to me or the boy dies."

"Don't say a word," Sticky whispered into Dave's ear. "He will remember your voice."

So Dave didn't say a word. Instead, he circled away from the treasure hunter, trying to maneuver closer to the boy.

"It's no use!" Damien hissed, circling, too. "Give it up and you'll both go free."

It would seem they were at an impasse. Dave would not give up the powerband, and Damien would not set Luis free without it. There was no escape, nor were there helicopters flying overhead on their way to rescue them.

And yes, Dave could have just disappeared down the face of the wall, but he felt responsible for the predicament that Luis was in. After all, it was his shoes and hat that had gotten Luis nabbed in the first place.

So this was a showdown.

A face-off.

A take-ten-paces-and-shoot situation.

And Damien Black, for his part, did not feel he could lose. Even if police swarmed the roof or helicopters arrived, he planned to escape undetected.

You see, the villain had brought along the Invisibility ingot.

All he needed was the powerband, and *poof*, he would simply disappear.

But what Damien Black had neglected to figure into his evil equation was the Sticky factor. For while the treasure hunter was keeping pace with Dave (the two of them moving round and round like figures on a deadly carousel), Sticky had whispered, "See you at home, *hombre*," in Dave's ear, and had snuck off of one ride and onto another.

In other words, he had sneaky-toed his way onto Damien Black!

Now, when Sticky made it up to Damien's collar, *he* wasted no time. With a wide-mouthed gecko CHOMP, he bit that evil *hombre* on the back of his neck.

"Aaaaghhh!" Damien Black cried, flailing backward and stumbling around like a madman.

For a moment, neither the Bandito Brothers nor Dave nor Luis thought anything of this behavior.

Damien Black *was*, after all, a madman.

But then Sticky shouted "Run!" at Dave, then deepened his voice and bellowed, "Get back to the mansion, you fools!" to the Bandito Brothers before chomping down on Damien Black's neck again.

To the Bandito Brothers, the voice sounded for all the world like it had come out of the mouth of Damien Black. But they knew that the boy in the sunglasses had something very valuable, so while Damien Black was screeching and flailing in pain, they charged Dave, thinking they could get whatever it was for themselves.

Dave looked around quickly but could see only one way out.

He grabbed Luis and simply said, "Piggyback." And, hoping desperately that the gecko power of Wall-Walker would hold their combined weight, over the edge they went.

Chapter 20
THE CAPPED CRUSADER

Dave did several smart things as he took Luis down the building.

First, he didn't go down the wall facing the pileup or the walls that faced the other streets. He went down the fire escape wall. The one that led to the narrow alleyway (where, if you'll recall, there were trash cans and mangy cats and broken bottles and not much else).

He also didn't take Luis all the way down.

He dropped him off at the fifth-floor fire escape landing.

"Wait!" Luis cried. "Where are you going? Who are you? How come you can walk on walls?"

Dave just flashed him the peace sign and scurried away.

The minute he was on the ground, Dave tore off his hat and sunglasses and stuffed them inside a trash can. Then he hurried back to the basement stairwell, whipped on his red sweatshirt, clipped on his helmet, and slipped back into the crowd.

He had two things on his mind.

First and foremost, Sticky.

Had Damien Black caught him?

Would he ever see his sticky-footed friend again?

But second, an alibi. He needed an alibi.

So he searched the crowd for Lily, and when he saw her, he went up behind her and stood like he'd been standing there all along. "Do you think he's going to come back down?" he asked.

"I hope so!" Lily said, glancing over her shoulder at Dave. "Wasn't that the most radical thing ever?"

"It sure was," Dave said.

So Dave established an alibi with Lily, but he

didn't stick around. He went back to his bike and rode home. Home, after all, was where Sticky had said he'd meet him.

But the little lizard didn't return.

Not that hour.

Or the next.

Or the next.

That night, Dave's parents (like everybody else in the city) tuned in to the news. When footage of Dave scaling the wall came on, Dave held his breath, hoping his parents wouldn't recognize him.

It was all so strange to watch.

Like it had happened in a dream.

Or to somebody else.

Then the newscaster said, "All through the streets, people were calling this capped crusader the Gecko. He scaled the wall like an enormous gecko lizard, rescued the boy, and enabled the police to capture his assailant."

"They caught him?" Dave asked.

"Of course they caught him," his father replied. "How did he ever expect to get away?" He pointed to the image of Damien Black, handcuffed and furious. "Look at that lunatic! I hope he spends the rest of his life behind bars!"

"Amen," Dave's mother murmured.

So Dave's parents didn't show any hint of recognition, which for Dave was an enormous relief.

Evie, however, was another matter.

First she stared at the TV.

Then she stared at Dave.

She stared at the TV.

She stared at Dave.

And although (for the first time in her life) she didn't point a finger or tattle, Dave could tell she was making plans.

Big, long-range, torturous plans.

But even that barely bothered him. All he really cared about was Sticky.

Where was Sticky?

He didn't sleep a wink all night. Every time he heard a tiny noise, he hoped it was Sticky. He checked the flower box outside the kitchen window over and over and over.

Sticky was never there.

In the morning, he left for school at the very last minute and even rode home at lunch to check the flower box.

Sticky had not come home.

"Where *are* you?" he whimpered, and in his heart of hearts he feared the worst. He even (for the first time) asked Mr. Kelly to please let his customers know that he was sick and couldn't do his deliveries (because he did, in fact, feel sick and didn't know how he'd make it through the afternoon).

He went straight home after school, and even Lily being friendly to him in the foyer couldn't raise his spirits. In fact, she depressed him all the more. "Everybody was talking about the Gecko today!" she said. "He's like a real-life superhero!"

A superhero?

He didn't want to be a superhero!

He didn't want to be the Gecko.

He just wanted *his* gecko.

Dave trudged up to his apartment, checked the flower box, then flopped onto his bed.

What was he going to do?

But then from beneath his pillow he heard, "Hey, *hombre*, you're squooshing me!"

"Sticky?" he gasped, whipping the pillow away.

"No, *señor*," Sticky said with a scowl. "You've got a talking pillow."

"Sticky!" Dave squealed, scooping him up. "I was so worried about you!"

"Easy, *hombre*, eeeeeasy! It was a long way, you know. And I was carrying something that slowed me down." He jumped back onto the bed and burrowed under the covers, and when he emerged, he had a coin in his hand.

A shiny coin.

With special notches.

He handed it over to Dave and said, "Here, *hombre.*"

Dave blinked at the coin. On it was the design of half a man. "Is it . . . ?"

Sticky gave a little gecko shrug and a little gecko grin. "Pop it in. See how you like it."

And so, with shaking hands, Dave did.

And disappeared completely.

Now, I could tell you what happened next. And I could explain how anyone who thinks that a simple cage is enough to hold a devilish villain like Damien Black has a lot to learn. But those are stories for another day.

For this story, for today, the time has come to say . . .

Adiós!

A GUIDE TO SPANISH AND STICKYNESE TERMS

adiós (Spanish / *ah-DEE-ohs*): goodbye, see ya later, alligator

amigo (Spanish / *ah-MEE-go*): friend, buddy, pal

ándale (Spanish / *AHN-duh-lay*): hurry up! come on! get a move on!

asombroso (Spanish / *ah-sohm-BRO-so*): awesome, amazing

ay-ay-ay (Spanish and a Sticky favorite): depending on the inflection, this could mean oh brother, oh please, or you have *got* to be kidding!

ay caramba (Spanish and a Sticky favorite / *ai cah-RAHM-bah*): oh wow! or oh brother! or I am not believing this!

ay chihuahua (Stickynese / *ai chee-wah-wah*): oh brother, oh man

bobo (Spanish / *BO-bo*): dumb, foolish, silly

bobos **banditos** (Stickynese / *BO-bohs bahn-DEE-tohs*): crazy bandits, stupid thieves

buenas tardes (Spanish / *BWAIN-ahs TAHR-days*): good afternoon

chimmy-chunga binga-bunga *loco***-berry burrito** (Stickynese): one crazy dude

chony baloney (Stickynese / *CHO-nee buh-LO-nee*): are you kidding?

creeping creosote (Stickynese / *CREE-uh-soht*): literally, oozing, thick, oily stuff derived from coal. But in Stickynese, holy smokes!

dios mío (Spanish / *DEE-ohs MEE-oh*): my God!

easy-sneezy (Stickynese): piece of cake, no sweat

estúpido (Spanish / *eh-STOO-pee-do*): stupid

freaky *frijoles* (Stickynese / *free-HO-lays*): literally, weird beans. But for Sticky, oh wow! or how strange!

hasta la vista (Spanish / *AH-stah lah VEE-stah*): see you later, goodbye

holy tacarole (Stickynese / *tah-cuh-RO-lee*): holy smokes!

hombre (Spanish / *AHM-bray*): man, dude

hopping (hurling) *habañeros* (Stickynese / *ah-bahn-YAIR-ohs*): literally, hopping hot peppers. But for Sticky, oh my gosh!

idiota (Spanish / *ih-dee-OH-tah*): idiot, dummy, someone who is *estúpido*

loco (Spanish / *LO-co*): crazy, loony

morrocotudo (Spanish / *mor-ro-co-TOO-do*): fabulous, wonderful

mucho lame-o (Stickynese / *MOO-cho*): *mucho* is Spanish for a lot or many, so *very* lame

ratero (Spanish / *rah-TAIR-oh*): thief

ratones (Spanish / *rah-TOHN-ays*): mice

señor (Spanish / *SEN-yohr*): mister

sí (Spanish / *see*): yes

siesta (Spanish / *see-EHS-tah*): nap, quick snooze

suavecito (Spanish / *swah-vuh-SEE-to*): suave, smooth, cool

tres (Spanish / *trays*): three